AF395920

Mary was born in Galway, Ireland and reared in the historic village of The Claddagh. She met and married her soulmate Declan, and the rest is history; theirs is a love that has inspired her and grounds her every day of her life. Described by her readers as a prolific writer, she can't imagine a day without writing. Fiction, being her greatest love, takes her into another world where she can decide where a story goes, often breaking her own heart and her words will grab you too.

I dedicate this book to my wonderful husband, Declan, a beautiful soul with a heart of gold. I will be forever grateful to the Gods that brought us together; he is my inspiration in life, my stronghold, and my best friend. Even after all these years together, we still dance in the kitchen.

Mary Finnerty-Morris

I HOPE PEACE FINDS HER

AUSTIN MACAULEY PUBLISHERS™

LONDON • CAMBRIDGE • NEW YORK • SHARJAH

Copyright © Mary Finnerty-Morris 2024

The right of Mary Finnerty-Morris to be identified as author of this work has been asserted by the author in accordance with sections 77 and 78 of the Copyright, Designs and Patents Act 1988.

All rights reserved. No part of this publication may be reproduced, stored in a retrieval system, or transmitted in any form or by any means, electronic, mechanical, photocopying, recording, or otherwise, without the prior permission of the publishers.

Any person who commits any unauthorised act in relation to this publication may be liable to criminal prosecution and civil claims for damages.

This is a work of fiction. Names, characters, businesses, places, events, locales, and incidents are either the products of the author's imagination or used in a fictitious manner. Any resemblance to actual persons, living or dead, or actual events is purely coincidental.

A CIP catalogue record for this title is available from the British Library.

ISBN 9781035841646 (Paperback)
ISBN 9781035841653 (ePub e-book)

www.austinmacauley.com

First Published 2024
Austin Macauley Publishers Ltd®
1 Canada Square
Canary Wharf
London
E14 5AA

Chapter 1
Look After My Little Angel

"Wake up, Tom—the alarm off—"

It was like a bad dream, a nightmare!

Moira had screamed, awakening baby Olivia, who continued to cry as she was held tight. Barely two years old, she would have no recollection of that awful day.

Tom had passed away in his sleep, there would be an autopsy, and she had frozen in her steps as she opened the front door to the concerned neighbours who had heard the screams.

Jenny, a middle-aged mother of three grown-up daughters, she couldn't do enough for you, and Brod, her husband, a quiet sort, always put Moira in mind of her own father, now too passed on.

It had been three years now since the accident that had taken her whole family. Her brother Mikey, the driver of the car, her mother, the front seat passenger and her dad, who always let her mother sit in the front on account of her being a bad traveller.

Mikey used to call her his co-pilot and they would laugh. It was a memory from hell, Tom was all she had now and of course, Olivia, the beautiful Olivia as Tom would always call her. Jenny and Brod were lovely neighbours, Tom had always lived there beside them.

After they'd married, they'd moved into his home with his mother. Although she'd had reservations about moving in, Moira had settled there in no time. Agatha, Tom's mother, was a lady and contrary to what she'd heard from people around her, including her own father who used to say, "If it's only two sticks against the wall, ye're better off on ye're own."

She'd been very happy living there, spoilt, in fact, she'd often thought. Had missed Agatha terribly when she had died. Tom had often told her about the times he'd spent next door as a child, himself and his brother, Frank.

Homemade bread with jam, happy hours playing in the garden with their dog 'Nutty', couldn't have picked a more suitable name, he was as mad as a hatter, Tom always said. A scruffy little thing he'd remembered, always biting at his heels but he'd loved to play with him.

Jenny and Brod had married very young, their mother used to say, they were childhood sweethearts, had a family of three girls, all grown up by the time Tom and Frank started to roam into their garden next door to play with the dog.

They'd love to see them coming, fussing about them and feeding them homemade bread and apple pie. Agatha, Tom's mother, said she'd often felt they were lonely, probably missed their own children; all having flown the nest by then and they'd had so much more love to give.

She would often shout over the back wall that she'd hoped the boys weren't a nuisance and they would assure her it was a pleasure to have them call by.

Moira loved to listen to Tom's stories, all in the past now, she would never hear his tender voice again, and Olivia, their only child would now probably not even remember the dad that had doted on her.

In fact, as it turned out, neither would she remember the warm touch of her mother, who'd fallen to pieces after her husband had died.

Shattered, she had gone on wearing a smile while inside she was broken. Until it all got too much and she'd left Olivia fast asleep in her car seat on the steps of the social services office miles away, the other side of the town.

She'd done her research and knowing that the office was about to open, she knew Olivia would be looked after better than she could look after her now, what kind of a mother would she make?

Shattered, going around in a daze with only thoughts of gloom going round in her head. The grief was eating her up. Olivia deserved better.

It wasn't a decision she had made overnight, she had thought about it for many a long lonely night after Tom had passed; it was too tough, she couldn't cope. She could no longer wear that smile. Tom, the love of her life, was gone. She too had died that day, she was just taking longer to die!

She'd waited across the road out of sight and watched as the office staff arrived one after the other, looking around to see if there was any sign of where the baby had come from.

Sounded like Olivia had slept through it all, Moira dared not think of when she would awake! A simple note attached to her pink cardigan read simply, "Look after my little angel; today, she is two."

Filed as abandoned with only the knowledge that she was two years old that very day, there wasn't much to go on where social services were concerned.

Reported missing after Jenny had knocked on the door a few times and missed her car outside, Moira would be found at the bottom of the river inside her car, still strapped in. The rear windows open, Olivia was presumed also missing but was never to be found, though many had searched.

Jenny and Brod questioned themselves for months as to why they hadn't seen this coming. Had they looked closer, would they have been able to help, maybe even avoid this catastrophe?

Why hadn't she come to them for help, she must have gone through a living hell to do what she'd done. Why had they not spotted that? It would eat them up for the rest of their days.

The news of the tragedy was all over the papers.

"Woman drowned, baby still missing."

Olivia had been placed with a couple for fostering, though assessed and deemed to be suitable, it hadn't worked out. Returned to the orphanage, she would take time to settle again, often crying for hours on end with no one consoling her.

"Maybe this will be the one," as Maggie packed her bag with Olivia standing up in her cot, looking on, she truly hoped that the couple due to pick her up within hours would be the ones to provide Olivia with a good home.

A social worker working for the agency, Maggie had seen a lot of coming and going in her time working there and had come to know some of the children. Mostly fostered into happy homes where some would be eventually adopted and become a part of a family again.

She'd often thought to herself if only she could bring them all home with her and love them, that was all they wanted really at the end of the day, someone to love them. Olivia was different though, always into herself like she was waiting for something or someone!

"Upsee Daisy!" She lifted the little girl up into her arms out of her cot and dressed her in pink. A beautiful child with baby blonde curls framing her face, big blue eyes bright as the stars of the night though as she looked up at her, there was a look of sadness in them.

Maggie had seen that look before in the eyes of children but rarely in one so young. Now called Angel because of the note attached to her cardigan when she was found, Maggie could feel the tension in her little body while holding her.

There was no doubt she was missing someone, someone who had loved her very much, her heart ached for her. All dressed and ready to go, Angel was asleep when the couple arrived to pick her up.

Having gone through the usual stages of fostering, they had waited anxiously for this day. With tears of joy in her eyes, Rose took her in her arms as Maggie held back her emotions.

"Good luck, little one," she whispered in her ear as she took her out of her cot, a dribble on her chin as she slept soundly.

Looking on as she cradled her in her arms with Billy, her husband, holding her tiny hand in his, Maggie just knew Angel would be loved and well cared for. She would call on them from time to time to see that everything was ok.

She'd spent many a day, wondering why someone would leave their baby on the steps of their office in a car seat to be looked after by somebody else, things must have been so bad and that mother or father must have been in a bad way to do something like that. It haunted her for a long time.

On her first visit to see how Angel was getting on, Maggie could see that she was settling in well and her foster parents were mad about her. Rose had told her that she'd slept most of the journey home that day while she had sat beside her in the back seat just looking at her.

When she awoke, she had cried the rest of the way, only settling down when she'd cried herself back to sleep again in her arms.

They'd had a room decorated as a nursery for her with unicorns on the wallpaper and everything pink including her wooden cot. Afraid that she might wake in the night and feel scared, they'd decided to move the cot into their room for a while, so that they could watch her and she wouldn't wake alone.

It had taken time for her to trust them but now she was beginning to with only the odd tearful look on her face. Rose had said she couldn't really explain it but sometimes, she would be playing with her toys on the floor and she'd go quiet, as if she was thinking of something and she would drop her lip, not cry out but a tear in her eye.

Maggie knew exactly what she meant, she had seen it too. Angel was missing someone, there was no doubt in her mind.

Jenny and Brod stood at the window and watched as the house next door was being cleared out, furniture, fittings, everything including the kitchen sink. As the big van pulled off, Jenny noticed they'd dropped something on the road, as she picked it up, she started to cry.

"Olivia had loved Cluedo, took him everywhere with her. Oh! Brod, it's all too much." She sobbed into the teddy until she'd cried her fill.

With Moira not having any family of her own, Brod had taken it upon himself to contact Tom's brother, Frank; he'd left his contact details with them after Tom's funeral, asking them to contact him should Moira need anything.

He'd only met Moira a couple of times but they'd hit it off straight away, they had become very close over the years and he could see that she was heartbroken, he wished he could have stayed longer after the funeral but he had work demands that had been put on hold while he took the few days off to bury his brother.

Hearing the news over the phone from Brod that Moira and Olivia were missing nearly floored him, he'd travelled the following day, leaving his workload behind. He'd told himself that he would leave no stone unturned until he'd found them.

He'd gone out with the life boats from dawn until dark, walking the floors while waiting for light again. Brod had asked him to stay with them though his bed had never been slept in throughout his stay.

He'd stand outside the front door, smoking at all hours of the morning and once daylight appeared, he was gone again. When Moira's car was discovered, his heart had sank; he'd had feelings for Moira more than he should have had.

He was ashamed to say he'd hoped when there had been no sign of it, that perhaps she had taken off with Olivia to live their lives somewhere away from the awful memories of that day. This was so hard.

That thought had crossed Brod's mind too when Jenny suggested reporting them missing, he'd held off reporting it for a few days hoping but Jenny had been convinced something wasn't right.

The baby's washing was still on the line and in talking to her in the few days previous, Moira had told Jenny that she had enrolled Olivia in a crèche down the road, she'd thought the company of the other children would do her good. She'd felt that maybe she was picking up on her sadness and it wasn't healthy for the child.

Jenny had felt for her that day, had asked her if she was doing ok and had told her that she and Brod would always be there for them. After all, Tom was like family to them. Moira had given her a hug and assured her that she was ok.

"Getting there," were her exact words. Jenny had pleaded with Brod, so what if they were wrong and they would turn up after having a trip away that would be wonderful.

But Jenny just knew something wasn't right, Moira would have said if they were going away. A tragedy confirmed Frank had taken as much time as he needed to come to terms with things, and had decided to put the house on the market, and the memories of his forbidden love would be kept within his heart but never forgotten, hence the furniture removal van that day.

Jenny would hold on to Olivia's teddy, it was all she had of them now. Olivia was still missing, presumed dead.

Maggie pulled up outside Rose and Billy's house and took a deep breath, she didn't know what it was about Angel but it got to her every time she came to visit. She'd always feel a bit hesitant when visiting children placed in foster homes, always feared the worst.

Maybe the child wasn't settling or the foster parents weren't happy, but with Angel, it was the look in her eyes when she'd come through the door, as though she was waiting for someone and the disappointment when it wasn't who she was expecting.

She wanted to ask her who it was she was waiting for, she wanted to pick her up and take her to whoever that was. It was obvious she was being well cared for, and loved. There was no question about that, Rose and Billy were over the moon to have her, even spoke of eventually applying to adopt her as their own.

Maggie was so happy to hear that, just there was something. Had Angel been older, she could tell them where her sadness was coming from, but because she was so young!

Do children remember the separation? The grief of parting from someone they love, so young? Do they carry it with them through their growing years festering inside of them? Or do they forget? Some may forget, Maggie thought to herself, Angel?

She wasn't sure, she seemed very deep. She would report Rose and Billy's interest in applying to adopt her as their own when she returned to the office and take it from there; it was early days, it would take time.

There was nothing in her files that would tell her where Angel had come from, no reports of family problems or ill treatment of the child, no involvement of social workers, nothing.

Was there a mother somewhere as heartbroken as the child she had left behind? Left with no option but to leave her.

Yet assuring she would be well looked after was she young, too young to bring up a child on her own?

Looking at the file over and over again, Maggie just couldn't get Angel out of her mind. She had come across some very sad cases over the years, abuse, alcohol, drugs. Children taken from homes where the dad had left and the mother was so out of it with drugs that she didn't even bat an eyelid to see the child go.

Neglect and even abuse, there were some very sad cases. This wasn't an easy career she had chosen but she loved it. It was at times tough but also very rewarding.

"Everything ok?" Pam had worked with Maggie since day one; more than a workmate, they had become very good friends. Often spent a night out offloading the sadness of the day. She stood beside Maggie's desk and waved a hand across her eyes, she was in another world.

"Hi Pam. Yes, I'm good, just you know, thinking!"

"How's she settling in? Angel?" Pointing to the file opened on Maggie's desk, Pam could tell that the look on her face wasn't a happy one, Maggie had something on her mind. A night out might be in order, they would meet for a beer at eight.

Both living nearby, they could walk to the nearest watering hole, wasn't the Ritz, but grand for a chat and a catch up. It was good to talk; working as a social worker, it was essential in fact!

"Have to go after this one, be wrecked in the morning." Pam left the beer on the table, they'd talked through the previous three beers and all was put to rights with the world.

Pam was right, it was their job to see to it that a child got a good home, getting involved other than checking up on things wasn't advisable after that. Angel would be fine, she would do her regular checks to make sure of that and be there should she be needed.

"Hi Rose, everything ok?" The phone was ringing when Maggie got to her desk.

Although having kept in touch throughout the time Rose and Billy had fostered Angel, this had been the first time in the nearly two years that had passed that Rose had come looking for her.

She was worried that something was wrong, it had been almost eighteen months since she had put through the application for adoption for them and had highly recommended them as adoptive parents for Angel.

"Oh! Maggie, I'm so excited I can hardly speak, the adoption has been granted, can you believe it? Can you believe it?"

Rose started to cry, she was so emotional, Maggie could feel herself well up.

"That's wonderful news, Rose. I'm so happy for you both."

"Yes, yes. Billy is here beside me, he's not able to speak, thank you Maggie, thank you for making our dreams come true."

There was no stopping the tears now, bring 'em on!

Maggie assured her that she was happy to help with the process but unfortunately, she would have had no part in the actual granting of the application, only to recommend them as suitable, which she had and which they clearly were.

Having had no record of Angel's parents only to say that she had been abandoned, her files would have had all the reports of Maggie's visits to Angel and her foster parents over the previous nearly two years. Maggie could never see the application being refused in the interest of the child's wellbeing.

She promised Rose that she would always be at the end of the phone should they need any advice or help in any way, she doubted she would be needed, Rose and Billy were such wonderful foster parents and would be wonderful adoptive parents as well.

She was so pleased for Angel, she'd had such a traumatic start in life, she deserved the best and Maggie was sure she would have that in Rose and Billy.

"Happy birthday to you."

Angel was five years old and officially the adopted child that Rose and Billy had waited so long for, they still looked at her in wonder and indeed often wondered why she had been abandoned.

Such a beautiful child, now running to Rose and Billy for a hug with a happy smile on her face, now calling out for dad in the night if she awoke from a dream, scared. Lips quivering, sobbing uncontrollably.

There was always a monster in the room, Rose and Billy could never make out where that idea came from. They'd never let her watch anything scary on TV, but she would hold on for dear life and cry herself back to sleep in Billy's arms, more often than not in Rose and Billy's bed.

First day of school looming, Rose took Angel shopping for new shoes. Beginning to get to know herself, Angel had sulked all the way home because she had picked a pair of shoes that she liked and her size wasn't available.

Rose had coaxed her into fitting on a different pair, which were far more suitable anyway, she thought, a perfect fit and very durable, she would get used to them.

A treat from the sweetie jar when they got home had brought back a smile to her face. As she played on the mat on the floor in front of her, Rose thought to herself, how quickly the years had gone by.

Far too quickly, she would start school in a couple of weeks, hopefully settle in easily. She wondered if maybe because she had been abandoned as a baby that it would cause her to feel insecure in any way.

She had noticed that if she or Billy had gone out, be it Billy going to work or herself going shopping or whatever and left her with one or the other of them, she would cling to the one that had been gone for a while when they got back, Billy had remarked on this too.

Hopefully, school would be a good experience for her, be with children her own age as well. Letting her outside to play wasn't something they had done as yet, firstly she was a bit young and probably, the main reason being that they were overly protective of her.

They would take her to the playground, which was only a short walk away and she really enjoyed that but she was always within sight of them.

As much as they were anxious of keeping her near, so was she, she would constantly look back to where they sat on the bench as if to make sure they were still there. She was their precious little girl.

The big day had arrived and it was decided that Rose would walk to the class with Angel while Billy would wait in the car in case there would be trouble finding parking. Every child that hopped and skipped up to the school were special to someone, none more special than the other.

Rose was in bits, it would be the first time that Angel would be separated from both of them, the very first time.

Her anxieties had reached a very worrying high! She hadn't slept, had walked the floors all night, checking in on Angel in case she too was anxious, she had slept the whole night through.

Were her anxieties unwarranted!

"Are you ok?" Billy had put his hand on hers, which was shaking as they got into the car. She smiled a nervous smile.

"She'll be fine," he assured her and off they went with a very quiet Angel in the back seat. Holding her favourite teddy in her arms, she watched as they approached the school, she had named her teddy Cluedo, Rose never knew where that name had come from but Cluedo went everywhere with her.

She was sure the school wouldn't have any objections to her bringing it with her, not on the first day anyway. She would explain it to the teacher, it would be fine.

"You look so beautiful in your new shoes, we are so proud of you, my darling." Rose lifted Angel out of her seat while Billy blew her a kiss, which she caught in her hands and planted on her lips awkwardly while still holding Cluedo.

"One for Cluedo, Daddy?"

Rose was struggling to hold back the tears, this was so hard, she didn't want Angel to see her being upset, that wouldn't do at all. Welcomed with open arms, the teacher was so lovely to them.

Angel held her mother's hand so tightly, it almost hurt; she was feeling strange, this was such a huge day for her. Told as nicely as possible, probably noticing that she was near to tears. Miss Hannah told Rose she could go and Angel would be fine.

Taking her by the hand, Miss Hannah proceeded to introduce Angel to another little girl called Katie who would be sitting beside her that day. Rose walked away, leaving a very unsure Angel with her lips quivering, she knew what was coming next and she wanted to take her home with her again.

It was a long few hours before she could pick her up again, Billy had said it was good that they hadn't heard from the school. Angel must have been ok or they would have contacted them.

Rose had secretly hoped that Angel would be missing her, that the school would ring for her to pick her up. She knew that having thoughts like that probably wasn't right but she liked that Angel was so attached to her.

She liked that she'd cling to her after she'd been out for a while, but she daren't tell Billy.

Chapter 2
Adopted

Right through preschool, into a big school as they would call it when a child left the preschool (even had a graduation day for the little ones), Angel had blossomed into a confident, bright young student.

She'd made friends and become very independent. As Rose and Billy looked on, there were days when they spoke about the times when she didn't want either of them to be out of her sight; selfishly, they sometimes wished for that side of Angel again, but that moment had now passed and so it should.

Their baby was growing up, they would have to get used to sharing her with the world. She had a lovely kind nature about her, a gift of making one feel comfortable in her presence, hence she would make friends easily.

Always in demand for birthday parties, days out with her friends always busy, but always had time for her mum and dad. She'd never go to bed at night without a cuddle and a genuine 'I love you'.

They were truly blessed to have her in their lives. Rose would still tidy her room and make her bed for her, though

Angel had often said she shouldn't, that they had her spoilt, but she liked to.

Often, she would take Angel's favourite teddy Cleudo, whom she still had on her bedside table and give him a cuddle, he too must be missing her, she'd thought to herself. All was as it should be, time was moving on and their little girl, who they loved more than life itself, was growing up.

Rose still wondered why she had been abandoned like that as a small child, she wondered about her birth mother and her dad.

Who did she take her good looks from and her pleasant way, she'd hoped perhaps she might have picked up some of hers and Billy's ways. They were after all nice sort of folk too, she thought to herself.

Billy had brought up the subject a few times now and Rose would keep putting it off.

"Angel needs to know that she was adopted, she's old enough now." Billy, with his best intentions at heart, didn't realise he was putting the fear of God in Rose. What if Angel wanted to look for her biological mother, her father? What if—?

She feared the worst!

"Nite nite, I love you." Angel was off to bed, oblivious to what was going round in Rose's head, they were the only parents she'd ever known, why complicate things?

She knew Billy was right but she wasn't sure that she herself was ready to share this information and she wondered if Angel was old enough to take it all in. They had promised to tell her when the time was right, it was the proper thing to do after all.

The right thing to do was easy back then when she was that cuddly little girl that didn't want to let either of them out of her sight, it was all in the distant future and didn't carry the fear that it carried now that the time had come.

Rose couldn't bear it if she wanted to look for her biological mother, Billy rightfully thought it was Angel's choice and a choice that they couldn't deny her. They would discuss it with her at the weekend, putting it off for another few days. Rose promised Billy that she agreed, although inside the fear was eating her up.

Her dreams would wake her in the night, dreams full of all kinds of terrible thoughts. Maybe getting it out there might bring her some peace of mind, maybe!

All cuddled up after her bath and snug as a bug in her fleece pyjamas, Angel sat to watch the TV, Rose watched her from the kitchen, knowing that the dreaded conversation was at hand, almost self-prophesying her reaction.

Billy washed as she dried the dinner plates, as they always did; they'd had many a good conversation while doing the dishes, many a good idea too in decorating the house or making changes.

He'd always say a dishwasher spoilt the art of conversation. Angel would sometimes put the dishes away and more often than not, there would be breakages. Things were about to change drastically now and Rose was very frightened.

Billy assured her that things would be the same but how could he know that and how could they be? Our little Angel, now eight years old was about to learn a new word. 'Adopted'.

"Look Dad, isn't she pretty?" Angel was pointing at the TV, there was an advertisement on for Communion dresses. With her First Communion day looming, she'd had all sorts of ideas about her dress.

One week, she'd want a long dress like a bride and the next, she'd want a dress that came to her knee. The young girl was wearing a knee length dress and she was very pretty indeed. If only that was the only thing on their minds, Rose thought, if only!

Billy sat beside Angel on the couch and she cuddled up to him as usual, a real daddy's girl. He called Rose to come and sit with them. Still holding the tea towel in her hand, Rose sat on the other side of Angel, almost holding her breath in fear of what she knew was to come.

Angel excitedly began to tell Rose about the pretty girl on the TV wearing the exact dress she wanted, "it was the exact one, Mum and she had the same hair too except she was prettier, I think."

Rose assured her that she was every bit as pretty and maybe even more so. Angel chuckled as Rose proceeded to tickle her.

The dreaded conversation had begun with Angel looking enquiringly from her dad to her mum. "Does that mean? Am I different to Katie?" With a tearful look in her eyes, she moved away from her dad as if she didn't understand and how could she, she was barely eight years old.

After hours of assuring her that she was no different to any other child in her class, she seemed to put it aside as the advertisement came on the TV again, "Look Mum, look."

She stood in front of the TV and wiped her tear stained face on the sleeve of her pyjamas. Rose was near to tears herself and just hugged her tight and promised to take her shopping after school next day.

Tucking her in that night hours after she'd gone to bed, Rose found her wide awake, staring out of the window. She lay down beside her and talked and talked until her inquisitive little mind gave in to sleep.

She wasn't sure if she'd understood what adoption meant and she wasn't sure if she was making a good job of explaining it either, it was tough and she was sleepy now.

Before she gave in to sleep, she turned to her mum and said in a very sleepy voice, "Do I have to be adopted? I don't want to be."

Rose cried her fill but not in front of Billy who'd thought it all went very well, she'd spent a while in the bathroom, hoping he would be asleep when she'd go into bed. It was all she could take for one day.

Next morning, Angel was full of the joys as usual with no mention of the conversation the night before, which they thought was a bit strange. She'd spoken about the Communion dress and how she was going to tell Katie (her best friend) that she was going shopping after school.

She was so excited. But on meeting her teacher in the hallway when picking Angel up from school, it was a different story, Angel had been upset on the yard but had cheered up again and didn't want the school to contact her mum when they asked.

It was so unlike Angel to behave in this manner, the teacher had said.

"Usually such a pleasant child, is everything ok at home?" Rose felt a bit intimidated by her question and wasn't in the mood to explain, wasn't the time or place anyway; she just wanted to see Angel now and see that she was ok.

Looking at her in the mirror of the car as she sat quietly in the back seat, Rose thought she looked a bit pale. "Are you ok, pet?" Angel responded with a hint of a smile and looked away again. She wasn't ok.

Rose would treat her to an ice cream in town, maybe after they'd had a look around for her dress, in case her hands would get messy. Wouldn't do to get sticky fingers on those beautiful dresses.

They'd had a lovely afternoon shopping and Angel was in great form, a different child to the one Rose had picked up from school. They would have to have a little chat when they got home, although knowing what was upsetting her was more than likely related to the conversation they'd had with her the night before.

Still, there was always the possibility that there may be something else the matter. Running straight to her dad, who was reading the paper sitting by the fire, Angel couldn't wait to tell him about her dress.

"It was the prettiest in the shop, it was even on the window." It had been on the window. That was where she'd spotted it, she'd stood looking at it while Rose had continued to walk towards the door of the shop.

Looking back to see where she'd gone, she could see her eyes filled with excitement and wonder. She quietly hoped it would fit and that it wouldn't be too expensive!

Turned out quite a bit more than she had intended to spend but looking at her in the dress and her face filled with joy, Rose would have spent every penny she'd had in her purse to get it for her.

As it happened, she had to scrape together the money for the ice cream as promised. They'd always got by but there was never much left over when all the bills were looked after, any extra expense in the week would be a struggle but she wasn't complaining.

Money wasn't everything; they'd had such contentment and happiness in their lives since Angel came into their lives that no amount of money in the bank could buy. Angel would have the dress of her dreams.

Billy came into the kitchen as Rose prepared dinner and gave her a hug. "Someone is happy," she agreed and decided to wait until Angel was in bed to talk to him about her concerns and indeed, the teacher's concerns about her in school that day.

He looked puzzled when she told him later on that evening, he'd thought Angel had taken the news very well and hadn't seemed to dwell on it too much. He hadn't been a bit concerned, hadn't even given it a second thought, she'd seemed her usual happy and bubbly self at breakfast.

Next morning, Billy brought up the subject of adoption again, in a sort of casual way, hoping to maybe gently get Angel to talk more about it. Understanding at the same time that a child's way of thinking was of course completely different to an adult.

He was thinking perhaps he hadn't gone about it the right way! What was the right way to tell a child they are adopted? That the only parents they'd ever known weren't in fact their biological parents at all.

Was there a right and a wrong way of telling a child this, all he knew was that Angel was a very intelligent child and he'd thought she was at the right age to be told, he wanted her to know that she was loved just the same as if she were their own.

It had been a long night twisting and turning, it had to be discussed and made to feel ok to talk about it, and they did. Angel ate her cereal and didn't say a word for a while.

With a dribble of milk on her chin, she smiled at her dad and put her hand on his as he reached for the butter. Billy, delighted to see her response, continued to explain how they'd waited so long for her and the joy that she had brought into their lives.

He wasn't sure if a child of eight would take this all in and understand it but one thing he did know was that he was wrong to spring it on her that night and expect her to take it all in.

There would be many a discussion about adoption, and as many questions as she had to ask as many times as she needed to ask them, would be answered. It was out in the open now and that's how it should be.

Billy and Rose were bombarded with questions in the days and months to come but that was ok and Angel was ok, which was the most important thing.

It was the night of her First Holy Communion and exhausted, Angel kicked off her lovely white shoes trimmed with lace and heels making a clicking sound as she walked. She'd loved them, ankle socks also trimmed with lace to match.

Rose had to help her to take her dress off as she sleepily and limply moaned that she was so tired. It had been a very long day with lots of treats and a little bit more spoiling than usual. They'd all enjoyed it and were all very tired.

They'd had a day off school the next day, so there was no rush in getting out of bed. Billy was pouring a glass of wine as she came downstairs; wasn't long before Rose had fallen asleep watching television, one sip of the wine and she had given in to sleep.

Maggie had been filing all morning and moaned as she picked up a file that had fallen on the floor. It was Angel's file. She stopped for a moment and began to think back on the little girl that had touched her deeply with the look of yearning in her eyes.

She wondered how she was getting on, it had been a while and normally, she wouldn't have much connection with a child once legally adopted but she did wonder about Angel. She knew she had found a happy home and adoptive parents that would love her as their own, as she was indeed their own now.

She wondered about her biological parents! Some cases just stay with you, she thought as she placed the file back in the cabinet.

"Can Katie come and stay for a sleepover?" Angel, now eleven years old (going on twenty-two), had really come to know herself of late. Rose couldn't remember being interested in make-up and boys at that age but things were different now, she'd thought to herself.

Nevertheless, she was still a child at heart and very vulnerable, hence the close eye that was kept on her movements and the company she'd kept.

Katie was a lovely young girl and had been a good friend to Angel all through school; in fact, Rose could see that Angel could run rings around her. She was a shy type of girl where

Angel would be more outspoken, not a bad trait once controlled.

Rose often thought to herself she'd not taken that from either herself or Billy. She too had thought of Angel's biological parents, how much they'd missed out on with such a beautiful child, ever grateful that herself and Billy had got the chance to have such a joy in their life.

Of course, Katie would be welcome to stay over anytime, they would giggle half way through the night and there would be pizzas bought in. Probably a make-up session and a modelling of Rose's not very modern wardrobe across the landing.

With high heels and falling over with laughter, Rose would join in with the fun and bring down some fancy hats that had belonged to her grandmother, that she could never part with although taking up half the attic space in boxes.

Every Christmas, there would be the same discussion as Billy shifted the boxes from one side of the attic to the other to get at the Christmas decorations, Rose would smile and remember her childhood.

They would go to their grandmother's every Halloween and dress up in her hats, she had a collection of hats going back for years, even had a maroon turban with a beautiful brooch at the front, lovely memories, very simple ways but much happiness.

Her childhood had been wonderful, she hoped they could give Angel happy memories as well and she would look back to her childhood and smile too.

Her mother always said a happy childhood was the foundation of a happy life, she wished Angel all the happiness in the world. Perhaps it would make up for the loss she had to have felt as a baby, probably forgotten now but somewhere, somewhere deep in her memory, she had lost the love of her mother and father.

She knew she could never replace that and that she wouldn't even try but she would get up every day and thank God for the opportunity to maybe give Angel a happy home and a feeling of being loved and cared for.

Coming to the end of their studies, both Katie and Angel were now qualified nurses, there would be a big night out planned for the weekend. Having supported her right through college, Billy and Rose would take great pride in watching her graduate.

Her whole life out ahead of her, the world was her oyster but Angel choose to apply for a nursing position at the local clinic where she would work as a public health nurse. Where had the years gone?

Not wanting to interfere, Billy and Rose had thought she would probably go abroad with Katie, who had great hopes of seeing the world with her qualification, but Angel had no ambition to go further afield as yet. Of course, it was her decision and her happiness was all that mattered.

One would never find happiness living someone else's dreams. She was happy with her interview at the clinic and even happier to have been successful in her application. Being from the area, she needed little training regarding the district; though not knowing everyone in the area, she would be familiar with the actual area.

She would be much happier working within the community as opposed to a hospital setting, she had told Katie. Though she would miss her dearest friend, they'd had different ambitions and would stay friends, no matter where they would end up; they'd made that promise to each other in their many discussions on the matter.

Katie had done her best to convince Angel of the bigger world out there and at times, Angel had questioned herself quietly, but she'd known all along where her heart lay.

Not knowing why she had chosen district nursing as a career, she'd just put it down to fate. A great believer that what was for you wouldn't pass you, Angel never questioned her gut feeling and always followed it.

A couple of months in the job and she'd known that she'd made the right decision, she would wake in the morning, excited for the day ahead, thankful that she was in a job that she loved.

Her patients became her friends and she was devoted to them, sometimes bringing home with her a worry about one or other of them not looking well or wondering if they were lonely in the night living alone.

Overwhelmed at times with compassion, she often cried all the way home, Rose would never pass remarks but always offered a shoulder to cry on. Though she would never discuss a patient with her mother, she would appreciate a hug after her day and maybe the odd tear on her shoulder.

Billy and Rose had bought her a little run around car, second hand unfortunately was as much as they could afford but she was so grateful and speechless on the day of her graduation to see it parked outside the gate. A red ribbon with 'Congratulations' stuck on the windscreen.

Both now retired, they would spend their days pottering round the garden, so proud of Angel, they would chat about her all the time over a cup of tea at eleven or a boiled egg at lunchtime, right up to going to bed at ten o clock.

Late nights a thing of the past, nine o clock would see them nodding in front of the TV until one of them would give the other a gentle nudge to say it was their bedtime. They were such a happy and contented couple, Angel being the centre of their lives since the day they brought her home.

Brought up to be a confident and caring child, Angel had never lost her kind nature even through college with nights out with her friends, she wouldn't let the night go by without ringing home before they'd go to bed to check that they were ok and bid them goodnight.

Growing up knowing she was adopted hadn't phased her in the least, she'd never felt any void in her life, she'd been loved and made to feel precious.

The phone was ringing as Rose opened the front door, she'd been shopping with Angel. It was the clinic, looking to talk to Angel, her name now shortened to Ang since Katie had started to call her that in primary school. Rose found it strange to hear someone call her Angel.

She was walking a few steps behind and as she entered the hallway, Rose handed her the phone.

"Hello, Angel speaking." There had been a district nurse taken ill and the secretary from the office in the clinic wanted a favour. Knowing how obliging Angel was, she had no doubt she would oblige and take her place for the rest of the week, although supposed to be on holidays!

"Of course I will." The secretary would organise for Angel's replacement to stay on her rounds for an extra week to cover. She'd been drafted in from an agency to cover Angel's holidays for a week.

Luckily, she hadn't planned to go anywhere for the week; it had been a very busy few months and she'd decided to just take the week and chill, but that could wait. She was new to this area and would have to go in to get instructions on how to get there and a list of the patients.

She would have to get up a bit earlier to call into the clinic on her way. It was in the next town the cover was needed, although having driven through it many a time, Angel had never even stopped in that town.

It was a pretty little village off the main road with hanging baskets outside the shop windows, of course she had got lost only five minutes from the main road.

Slowing down at every corner to read the names on the streets, she was late for her first patient but she understood when she explained that she wasn't familiar with the area.

Working down through her list of patients, she hoped she had given enough of her time to each one. A stranger to them all, she tried to make them feel at ease, she always liked to give as much time as she could to all of her own patients.

She thought it was important to make them feel cared for and special. At times meaning she would be a couple of hours late getting home but that didn't matter. Her last call was to an elderly lady bedridden and being cared for by her elderly husband.

Looking in her notebook, she hoped she was at the right address, she'd counted the numbers on the doors as she'd gone down the road. There was ivy growing wildly all over the front of the house, covering the number of the house.

Every other house had their numbers plainly to be seen on the right of the doorway but not this one, it was hidden under the ivy. Getting her bits together, Angel read her notes and approached the front door.

Looking round the garden, she could tell it had been indeed loved and cared for but by the look of things, had been left to its own devices of late. It was planted with the most beautiful shrubs but had over grown.

Perhaps she'd thought the lady she was about to visit was no longer able to tend to her garden, perhaps her husband used to look after it and was no longer able. It looked sad and neglected with the ivy almost covering the door at this stage.

Soon, she would know the story; she hoped things were ok inside. Angel always found herself a bit apprehensive when visiting a new patient, always hoped she would make a good impression, come across as caring, no matter what the situation might be.

She remembered her first day on the job, she was physically shaking as she dressed a patient's leg. Although confident that she was doing the right thing and making the patient feel at ease as was so important when working as a nurse, inside she was feeling physically sick.

She wondered if maybe her patient was waiting inside just as anxious as she was. After all, she wouldn't be familiar with her, she would probably be used to having the other nurse that had taken ill.

With a deep breath and a little chat to herself that she'd got on well with the other new patients on this route, and there was absolutely no reason that she wouldn't get on with this lady that she was about to meet, Angel rang the bell.

It took a few minutes to get an answer but once she got an answer, she realised straight away that her fears were unfounded.

You couldn't meet a nicer couple than Jenny and Brod. Angel was made to feel at ease right away, it was almost like she'd been there before, with these people before; it was a strangely familiar feeling. She smiled as the gentleman introduced himself.

A lovely gentle name for a lovely gentle lady, Jenny. As her husband opened the door and introduced himself as Brod, she was warmly invited in. There was very little to be done for Jenny, she was sitting like a lady with a smile on her face when Angel went into the room.

Her husband had all the work done, in apologising for being late and remarking on him having all the work done, Angel was told politely that looking after Jenny was his pleasure, and handed her a nice cup of tea and a chocolate biscuit.

She was starving, hadn't stopped all day, so she really appreciated the gesture. A chair was pulled over beside the bed and Angel was told to take the weight off her feet for a while.

Turned out Jenny enjoyed the little chats with the nurses who called, she'd broken her hip a few years back and hadn't recovered from it as well as was hoped, they'd put it down to brittle bones, she'd said with a frown.

Brod carefully handed Jenny a cup of tea as well and a chocolate biscuit. He would pop down to the shop if that was ok while she was there, Angel had smiled and told him to take his time, she was in no hurry at all.

She had never seen so many family photographs as was on the bedroom wall. Jenny went on to name all of them; they'd had three daughters, all living abroad with their families.

There was a sort of sadness in her eyes as she spoke, a longing. Then her smile returned as she spoke about her grandchildren, had twelve grandchildren; four boys and eight girls.

They would come to visit on summer holidays and Christmas, you could see she would like to have seen more of them, maybe be more a part of their lives. Brod was back again in five minutes with a few groceries in his bag.

As Angel got up to go, Jenny put her hand out to her and they shook hands. She assured her she would call by again within the week as she was covering for the rest of the week at least.

Getting out of the village was twice as confusing as finding her patients within the village, it was like a maze! Turned into dead ends four times before she eventually found the road out, she was happy to be on the main road again.

It had been a long day and she was looking forward to an early night and maybe a bath, her feet were sore. Rose had a roast dinner ready for her when she got home, having eaten earlier, she was keeping Angel's plate hot in the oven.

Angel appreciated how well off she was, having her dinner handed up to her every day and not alone that, but her laundry was taken care of as well. As often as she would tell her mother to leave the laundry and she would look after it, she still cleared the basket every day.

All fresh and clean and ironed to perfection left on the end of her bed. She was so lucky and always showed her appreciation only to be told, "Sure, what else have I to do, passes the time for me," and Rose would wink at her.

Another early morning call from the office as Angel was about to leave for her days' work, the nurse she had been covering for had requested leave indefinitely. Angel had been getting on so well in that area that the secretary wondered if maybe she would be happy to work there for a bit longer.

It would, of course, be her choice but thought she would offer it to her first as she was already familiar with the route. Of course, she wasn't forgetting Angel had given up her holidays to oblige her over the last couple of weeks but she would look after her when things got a bit quieter if that was ok with her.

There was no problem there, Angel was happy to stay covering for as long as she was needed though she missed her old patients from her regular area but she would get back there again, she was sure.

As for the holidays she was owed, there would be plenty of time to take them; she would maybe organise a few days extra with her Christmas break.

Rose had packed a lunch with homemade brown bread and tomatoes, Angel loved her tomatoes, would have one in her hand and eat it like an apple when she was younger, loved them. Her favourite smell would be tomatoes frying, she would come in the door with her nose in the air, smiling, if Rose was frying tomatoes.

A quick kiss on the cheek and she was off on her way, her lunch box under one arm and her car keys along with her bag, all checked and filled with supplies the evening before at the clinic ready for her patients, under the other.

She was always busy, always running. Rose would worry that she was doing too much, too obliging. She often felt as much as she loved her job and would go out of her way for anyone, perhaps she was sometimes too obliging.

"People can take advantage too," she would say to Billy as they would wave her off at the door.

To which he would reply with a grin, "She's fine, stop worrying," but that wouldn't stop her! Angel would always leave Jenny until last to call on, it gave her more time to chat when she had looked after her other patients.

Once she was happy that they were all sorted and comfortable, her time was her own. She could spend hours chatting to Jenny, she was such an interesting person and so, Angel wasn't sure what but there was something special about her, something almost familiar.

In so short a time, they had become friends. She used to say "Angel by name and angel by nature," and always shook her hand when she was leaving, she had such a soft gentle touch.

It was coming up to Christmas and the coldest December she had ever remembered. One by one, the Christmas trees were appearing in the houses of her patients, all alight, sparkling, a feast for the eyes.

Angel loved Christmastime. Though an adult now, she would be up at six o clock in the morning, hoping for snow outside the window (that never came) with excitement for the day ahead.

She'd felt it was an opportunity as well to spoil her parents, though adoptive parents they were the only parents she'd ever known. Sometimes, she wished she could remember back but not a memory in the world, only of Rose and Billy and how they'd spoilt her down through the years.

She was so lucky. She did have one keepsake from her past, Rose had given it to her when she was sixteen. "Old enough now to appreciate," were her words. In opening the envelope inside the box and reading what was inside it, Angel had looked up at her mother, baffled.

'Look after my angel'; was this supposed to mean something to her? Rose had explained how this note had been pinned to her cardigan when she was left in the care of the social services that day, they'd reckoned by either her dad or her mother.

Distraught, no doubt, in having to make that awful decision. She'd also been given the outfit she'd been wearing that day, by Maggie the social worker who'd said she'd thought the day may come when Angel would look for some connection with her birth mother and that was all they had to offer.

Angel had taken the box with the note and gone to her bedroom. She would take it out every now and then in the privacy of her bedroom and smell the little cardigan and kiss the note. It wasn't much but it was something and she was glad that Rose had given it to her.

She would have been oblivious to its being, Rose needn't have kept it for her but it was the right thing to do and after she had come to terms with it, she cherished it. She did wonder often but where could she go with her curiosity, nowhere!

Christmas came and went in a flash, the holidays were a welcome break and Angel felt she needed it. She'd been owed a few days as well, so it was a lovely break. On her return to work, sadly she'd learned of the passing of one of her elderly patients; Barbara had been very ill for quite some time.

Angel had only come to know her of late when she was posted in that village to cover the regular nurse on sick leave, she was a lady. With all her calls finished for the day bar one, she sat into the car with a sigh of relief, there was just Jenny now and she really enjoyed that visit, and then home.

She longed to take her shoes off, they were pinching her small toe, she wasn't sure why she'd had them for years though hadn't worn them much. Jenny was her usual smiling self, Angel didn't know what it was but it felt like going home every time she called on Jenny.

Seemed somewhat familiar though it couldn't be, she'd only come to know Jenny recently and hadn't even driven through that village until then, never mind her house. How could it feel familiar!

Brod took his shopping list and his little carrier bag and off he went to do the shopping while Angel was sitting with Jenny. There was a beautiful bunch of flowers beside her bed. "Is it your birthday, Jenny?"

Angel stood beside the flowers to smell them, she loved fresh flowers, there was a card signed 'Frank', no message just 'Frank'. Jenny went on to tell her that Frank had been a neighbour many moons ago, worked abroad now but had been back on a bit of business and called by with the flowers, had said he will call again before he goes.

Angel thought that was so nice but wasn't a bit surprised, Jenny had such a lovely way about her not one you would forget easily, it was no wonder he had called by to see her. She hoped as she herself went through life that she might be remembered as being a kind person, one to give of her time generously.

One that might have made a difference! Jenny looked deep in thought, so Angel left her in peace, there were a few dishes in the sink, so she busied herself until Brod returned. Told that there was no need to be doing dishes and that it wasn't her job, Brod offered Angel a cup of tea and a nice piece of chocolate Swiss roll.

It was Jenny's favourite, he'd wanted to cheer her up, had said that it had been a hard day for her, talked about Frank and the visit and the flowers and how it had brought back so many sad memories to her. She'd cried for hours after he'd left.

Not wanting to seem nosey, Angel had left it at that. Brod had said no more on the issue nor had she. It was a lovely spring evening and Angel's head was filled with thoughts of Jenny on the way back home, there were a few words that had stuck in her head that Brod had said about Jenny.

Chapter 3
Jenny

"I thought she might die under the weight of it," he'd said, handing Angel her Swiss roll.

Whatever it was had stayed with her all these years, many moons ago as she had said herself. Rose would always ask her about her day while sitting at dinner, she would never discuss her patients just tell her that it had been either a difficult one or it had gone well.

She was tired and a bit bothered about Jenny, she hoped she would have a good night's sleep. Brod was such a good husband, you could see how much he cared for her in the way he talked about her with concern in his voice.

There were times when she found her work hard, even emotional at times but always rewarding. She got to meet people every day, the nicest of people, only ever wanting a little bit of care and attention and so very grateful for her time, her caring and a lot of the time, just a little bit of company.

Though a well-paid job, it wasn't about the money for Angel, it was about bringing comfort to someone in pain when her dressing was embedded in her leg ulcer, gently removing it while keeping her in chat and her mind off her pain.

It was about changing a bed that the old man had slept in all night, sopping wet because he'd lost the sensation of realising he needed the toilet. It was about dignity when there was little else to offer and it was about providing as best she could a jolly end of days to those whose end was eminent.

She often wondered what life was about, people working hard all of their lives, only to end up depending on strangers sometimes to help them with the most basic of tasks, the lucky ones having family members to take care of them in their old age.

Old age should be honoured, she'd thought to herself, driving along next morning, only to be brought back to reality with a bang; she'd had a blowout. With not a clue what to do, she was only grateful that the road was quiet and she hadn't been hurt; she would have to call the recovery service.

Looking at her watch, she was glad she had left a bit early though she would still be running late. The recovery service arrived fairly quickly and she was on her way within the hour. A very nice lad had repaired her car swiftly, taking off the old wheel and replacing it with the new one.

Angel was so glad he'd known where to find it as she didn't have a clue where it was. He'd given her a lovely smile and was so pleasant. With apologies to all, she got through the day, arriving home late again.

Billy was a bit worried to hear what had happened and took the damaged wheel to be repaired next day, calling on Angel while fitting it in the boot just for future reference, they'd had a laugh.

Rose was a bit concerned that Angel was looking tired, she would see to it that she put her feet up and rested when she came home.

Normally, she would be fussing over her and her dad, making sure there was firewood in for the fire so that they wouldn't have to go outside in the cold in the morning. Or doing the shopping on the way home to save them having to go to the shops; she would ask every day if they needed anything and never came home without it if there was something they needed.

Often picking up a nice chocolate cake as well, not that they expected her to be dancing attendance on them and she holding down a full time job as well. A very demanding job it was, she just thought she looked tired, she'd only have her dinner eaten when she'd be falling asleep in front of the TV.

Rose thought to herself it was bad enough herself and Billy nodding off after the dinner but Angel was young, she should be out with her friends, enjoying herself. The weekends were the same, she would be off for the couple of days but spent her time doing stuff around the house.

Rose would be told to put her feet up that she'd been cooking her dinners all week long and Angel would take over for the weekend. She was such a beautiful girl with the loveliest way about her, surely one day she would meet someone nice.

If a boyfriend was ever mentioned, she would just laugh. There was a bitter cold breeze as Angel loaded her dressings into the boot of the car outside the clinic, and just as she was getting into the car, fumbling with her keys, her hands were so cold she could hardly hold them, the receptionist called her back into the clinic; there was a call for her.

Rose was on the phone, her dad had taken ill and she was very upset. She had called the doctor and the ambulance was on the way. Angel did her best to calm her mother and assured her that she would be straight home once she'd organised cover for her calls.

It was immediately organised and Angel was on her way home, her heart thumping in her chest in fear of what she was about to see. Billy had never been sick, in fact Angel could never remember her dad even going to the doctor.

If he came down with flu or indeed a pain or ache anywhere, he'd fob it off and say, "Sure, ya have to die of something."

Tears rolling down her face, she pulled up around the corner, she would wipe her tears and be strong for her mother. A thought that would be short lived, soon as she'd seen her mother in such a state, her heart broke for her and soon the tears were rolling again.

The doctor had been with her dad for a good few minutes, her mother had said, white as a sheet and shaking. Angel hugged her and told her everything would be ok; after all, he'd been so healthy all his life apart from the odd arthritic twinge in his shoulder, diagnosed by himself.

She would make a cup of tea and await the doctor's return from their bedroom where Rose had found him struggling to breathe when she brought him his breakfast on a tray. He'd seemed tired the night before, so she had decided to leave him in bed and take him up his breakfast as a treat.

Little did she know the state she would find him in, she hadn't noticed anything out of the ordinary when she got up in the morning, he seemed sound asleep.

On his return, the doctor seemed deflated, Billy was a lifelong friend of his and though he didn't attend the surgery very much; in fact not at all, they'd often met for a pint and a natter. There was nothing he could do, it was a bolt out of the blue, he'd said, Billy was gone.

As the ambulance pulled up outside, Angel felt sick, it was too late, all too late for her beautiful dad, the only dad she'd ever known; though not her biological father, he'd given of himself unselfishly all of her life.

This was the worst day of her life, what would her mother do without him, they were joined at the hip. People used to say of them that if one sneezed, the other would catch a cold.

Of course, they'd had their ups and downs like any married couple but Angel always quietly hoped that if one day she was married that she would be lucky enough to find a man like her dad.

She was trying to remember her last words that she'd had with him, it had been the evening before they'd chatted at dinner. He'd said it was so nice to have had the dinner with her on a week night, she was always so late getting home that they'd have had their dinner before she'd come home and she would eat hers on her lap in front of the TV.

It was only a few weeks previous that he'd bought her a lap tray, so that she could eat with comfort in front of the TV. He was so very thoughtful.

She remembered when she was in college and she used to cycle there and back even on the wettest of days. He would service her bike regularly and almost daily check the tyres in case they needed air and if it had rained, he would be waiting at the front door to put a plastic bag on the saddle of the bike, so that it would be dry when she came out after her lunch.

Rose would indeed be lost without him, things would be so different now; they were different already. The house had a sort of eeriness about it all of a sudden, a quietness, a loneliness. Was this death, cold almost scary cold like he'd been stolen and left a cold breeze in his wake?

The silence was deafening, the immediate feeling of loss immense. In the days and weeks that followed, distraught and numb, Angel and her mother had to carry their grief stricken hearts with courage, weighed down; there would be days when their burden was almost too heavy to bear.

But there was work to be done, affairs to be sorted, though Billy had put his affairs in order years since he'd had one wish to be carried out after he'd left his beautiful Rose. He'd wanted her to walk on proudly, having shared her life so selflessly, having given Angel the love and care that only a mother can.

His days had ended, his letter read but she must be strong and live the rest of her days out without him now. He would wait for her in that special place that they often talked about, Rose had sobbed from the moment the solicitor started to read the letter Billy had given him only a short time before.

There hadn't been a word said in the car on the journey home until they'd pulled up outside the house, Rose had sat, looking into the house as if she didn't want to go in. Angel put her hand on hers and squeezed it.

"Do you think he knew? I mean, the letter—did he know he was going to leave us soon?" Nodding her head, Angel felt so exhausted, so lost she didn't really know what she thought any more.

One thing for sure she now knew the pain of loss, she'd attended many a patient's funeral and felt, well she'd thought she'd felt their pain of the loss of a wife or a husband but this was something else.

She ached from head to foot, she wanted to feel his mighty hug once more, hear his voice that which had soothed her in her childhood and so many times reassured her growing up.

She wanted her dad and she wanted things back to the way they were, she always knew she had been lucky in being so loved, she'd never taken it for granted and always appreciated.

But that was of no comfort to her now, she had never felt such sadness and was of very little comfort to her mother at this time when she needed her the most. Time would move on regardless of their loss, their heartbreak. Angel would get up in the morning and get organised for the day ahead because that's what had to be done.

There were days when she would just as happily stay in bed, laze around and wonder what it was all about. There was Rose, grieving until she could cry no more, having to push herself to get up in the morning and do her bits around the house, she was lost.

She had given her life to Billy and spent her days doing for him as though they had been joined at the hip. There was never a decision made on their own, never a plan made without involving the two of them and Angel, of course. What was it all about? Life!

One thing she knew in watching Rose fall to pieces was that she would never get involved with a man and become so dependent on him that without him, life would be meaningless, empty.

As she took the little pink cardigan out of the box and read the note attached, 'Look after my angel', she got a shiver down her spine. She had often taken the box down from the top of the wardrobe and smelled the cardigan, which had a certain smell and she wondered if maybe it would have been a scent of her birth mother.

It sort of comforted her, especially now having lost her father, she'd found herself thinking about her birth mother a bit more since Billy had died.

It had never caused her to shiver before, perhaps it was her state of mind, she felt anxious, she wanted to talk about Billy but didn't want to upset Rose.

Driving up towards Jenny's house, her day almost done, Angel started to cry uncontrollably; it was like a dam had burst. She pretended to be reading her notes in case Brod might be looking at her from the window, she had to compose herself.

She was attending a patient, what was she thinking of? But it had just come out of the blue, taken her by surprise. As if they knew she'd been upset, Brod and Jenny had chatted so compassionately with her for ages.

They were such nice people. Brod had the work done as usual and the tea was made as soon as she came through the door. She so enjoyed her visit with them, they'd become friends more than Jenny being a patient.

Theirs was another relationship that Angel feared their parting would leave the other one crushed. She hoped it wouldn't be for a long time yet but they were both in their eighties, it was inevitable, inescapable. Such was life! They'd chatted about Billy as if they'd known him and enquired as to how Rose was doing.

It was just what Angel had needed, someone to talk to. She'd felt a weight lifted, she would bring a nice chocolate cake home to Rose. The one that Billy liked and they would talk about the happy times, of which there were many.

Maybe she wanted to talk as much as Angel did but didn't want to upset her! The kettle was put on the boil and the old box of photos were taken down, they both sat on the sofa and the box was left between them.

Years of memories, they laughed and they cried but mostly, they remembered Billy; with lighter hearts, they rose their cups of tea to him and enjoyed his favourite chocolate cake.

As she kissed her mother goodnight, Rose thanked her daughter for taking the time to talk, for bringing her back down memory lane. It would be a night that would initiate the healing process for both of them. Albeit a long and painful process but a step in the right direction.

When she called on Jenny after the weekend, she had company, so as not to intrude, Angel told Brod at the door that she could call back later when their visitor had gone. Brod wouldn't hear of it, seems Jenny had spent the afternoon talking about her lovely nurse and was anxious for Frank to meet her.

It was the Frank that had sent her the flowers, Angel remembered his name on the note attached. She remembered Jenny had been quite upset after receiving the flowers but hadn't said why and Angel wasn't going to ask.

He'd given Jenny what Angel thought or assumed was a get well card that day, it was an envelope anyway and she was upset again when she'd opened it.

Maybe she was just thinking back to happier times when they'd lived next door. He was a really nice guy in his fifties, she reckoned, had lovely manners too; she always looked for manners in people, she thought it was one of the most important traits in a person.

He'd introduced himself, getting up from his chair and asking her to sit down, that she must have been tired after her day. They'd chatted for a while and it was as if she'd known him all of her life when she left, it was a strange feeling, there was no uneasiness about his company.

Which was unusual for her, she would be all anxious normally in a stranger's company, especially of the male sort! She hadn't had much experience with men nor did she desire to have! Her life was just fine as it was, her patients, and her weekends shopping with Rose, sure there wasn't any time for socialising.

Her favourite thing to do after her day's work was to curl up in front of the TV in her pyjamas and snooze through the film she had looked forward to watching, and never got to see. Jenny seemed so happy to have Frank there, seems he'd spent a lot of time with them as a child when he'd lived next door with his family, he'd had a brother who had died young.

They would both have played in the garden with the dog.

The kettle was still warm but no sign of Rose when Angel got home, she wondered where she'd got to. Wasn't like her not to have her dinner in the oven, lovely smells of whatever she'd cooked, it was always something wholesome and warm after her day.

Rose was a great believer in a hot meal at the end of the day to keep one going. If something had happened to her, she would have been notified surely, but she hadn't called in to the clinic today, she was running late on account of having a chat with Jenny and Brod and their guest Frank.

She'd decided to do her notes at home and drop them in the following day, there had been nothing out of the usual on her round, so it would be fine. She didn't like being in the clinic when everybody else had gone home and they would have shortly after she'd arrived, she'd always found it a bit creepy being left there on her own and having to lock up.

It was a big place with lots of creaks, she'd jump every time a door would creek and it often would because of the draughts. Before she'd got time to worry, which wouldn't take long (she was a proper worry worm), Rose came up the path in a panic.

She'd had a good idea, she'd said, it being a nice sort of a day, she thought it would be nice to get some fish and chips for tea. Thinking she would be there and back in no time as it was only up the road, she hadn't thought to leave a note for Angel, thought she'd be well back by the time she'd got home.

But alas, when she saw the queue meeting her as she turned the corner, she had nearly passed out, but she hadn't prepared anything else for dinner, so she would wait it out. When she saw Angel's car outside the gate, she panicked, she would be worried and that was the last thing she wanted.

Angel assured her that it was fine and not to worry as long as nothing had happened to her, she hadn't even begun to worry about her, she was only in the door in front of her. The fish and chips were delicious and it was a lovely idea, Angel had said to her mother with a smile, they'd sat in the porch and talked about the day.

Angel had spoken about Frank, Jenny's guest and how he was such a gentleman and how it was so strange how she'd felt as though she'd met him before. Up early next morning, Angel was first into the clinic, got her notes in order, picked up her dressings for the day and was off on the road again.

It was a beautiful day, the early mornings were the best time of the day, she thought to herself. So much wasted time lying in bed in the mornings, she promised herself she would get up early on her next day off and make the most of the day, as if!

Her first call was Mrs Mc Dee, a lovely woman bedridden with bedsores on her back; to her disbelief, Angel had been met at the door by her son Jacob, who'd informed her that his mother had been admitted to hospital by her doctor during the night, suspected hernia.

Had awoken in the night doubled in pain. Jacob had just come back to get a few bits for her and intended leaving a note on the door for the nurse as instructed by his mother. She had been given medication and was comfortable when he'd left her but would have to stay for a few days to see how she would go, she wasn't impressed at all, he'd said, smirking.

He'd looked tired, probably up all night with her. Even though her first name was Eithne, everyone just called her Dee. Jacob was her only child; well, he was an adult now but he adored the ground she'd walked on. Angel could only imagine the thoughts going round in his head, watching his mother in pain.

The day didn't improve after that either, her old man Charlie, the only male on her round had knocked his leg off the pedal of the bike and had broken the skin, it looked very sore indeed.

Dressed and made to feel as comfortable as possible, Angel continued on her way, making a note of contacting the hospital to arrange an appointment for Charlie to attend for a check up on his leg; she hoped it wouldn't turn nasty or end up being a leg ulcer.

He was a gentle old soul, living alone and though advised to rest and elevate his leg, she knew in her heart and soul he had no intention of doing; so, he would be at the market on Saturday morning to buy fresh flowers for his wife's grave as he did every Saturday.

Not long gone, he'd missed her so much and had talked about her on every visit to him. It was evident that they had been soul mates, no children as they were late in life getting married but content with their lives as they were.

He always seemed to have a tear in his eye, Angel thought, she wasn't sure if it was maybe a blocked tear duct or maybe an allergy or perhaps it was just loneliness, a sadness that never went away.

There were days when she just wanted to take her patients home with her and look after them all, so that they would never be alone again. As she pulled up outside Jenny and Brod's house, she noticed a car in the driveway, it was the same car that had been there the day they'd had a visitor in the last week as well.

Angel thought to herself that it must be Frank's car, although just having met him once, she felt a familiarity about him. Brod was standing at the front door and guided her straight into the bedroom; she could see she had been right, Frank sat at Jenny's bedside and they were laughing their heads off, it was so nice.

Getting up to go as she left her bag on the chair beside Jenny's bed, Frank smiled as he passed her by. Jenny started to explain what they had been talking about and what they'd been laughing about, they'd been reminiscing, had travelled back years in time all still vibrant in their memories.

Sounded like they had been the best of friends, Angel thought, it was doing Jenny the world of good having Frank around; she was bright eyed and almost excited as she spoke about him.

Rose was sitting in front of the TV when Angel got home and she'd been crying, she was missing Billy. Of course, Angel missed him too, of course she did but she'd had her work as a distraction, it was harder on Rose, she was pottering around the house, alone most of the day.

She'd tried to hide the tears but the tell-tale signs were very obvious, her eyes were swollen and her make-up was running down the sides of her face. "Time doesn't heal," she'd said. "It just helps you to accept it."

She'd wiped her eyes in her apron and proceeded to take the casserole out of the oven, it smelled glorious and Angel was starving.

They'd chatted over dinner with Billy being the topic of conversation the whole evening, hugging her mother on the landing as they went up to bed, Angel could feel herself well up but held back the tears until she got into bed where she'd cried herself to sleep.

Another day tomorrow, she would have to stay strong, she would take Rose to visit Billy's grave at the weekend and maybe have lunch out for a treat, they both deserved it.

The grave looked already a small bit sunken, the flowers laid recently withered. It had rained constantly over the last week and Rose had put it down to that.

"No flowers could withstand that awful rain—ruined," she'd said, looking down at them sadly. The man she had loved for so long, her strength, her soul mate now buried beneath the sunken earth, she'd cried until she'd had no more strength in her.

There would be no tidying of the grave today. Angel would come back another day and tidy it up, bring fresh flowers and throw away the wilted ones.

The flowers sent by friends and neighbours had been so beautiful on that awful day, Angel remembered just staring at them as if in a daze. Numb with grief and disbelief, the beauty of the flowers had lodged in her memory.

Sitting in the coffee shop opposite Rose, she'd thought she'd looked old and sad, probably prefer to be sitting in her kitchen but Angel wanted to treat her, neither of them in the mood though.

Checking her list for her round next day, she noticed her patient Dee was back on her list, she had been discharged from the hospital and given medication for her hernia.

In speaking to her son Jacob at the door when she called, he'd told her that the hernia was too close to her heart to operate, so she would be on a very strict diet in line with her medication.

She wasn't very impressed with her diet, she'd loved her sticky buns and crisps, not to mention chocolate bars. Angel chatted with her for a while and checked her bedsores as was her reason to call in the first place, they hadn't improved any since she'd last attended her, if anything they seemed more sore and tender.

Jacob was such a caring son, danced attendance on her morning, noon and night, not an easy task. His mother, although a lovely person, was hard work, always criticising her son and finding fault in his cooking and cleaning around the house, nothing was ever done right.

Now a few months attending Dee, Angel could never say she'd been neglected in any way or her house either. It would be spotless, although she could understand her frustration in not being able to do for herself, Angel thought to herself.

"You don't know how lucky you are to have your son living with you and looking after you so well." There would be many that envied her.

Many with no one to care or look after them, many who would spend their days waiting for their nurse to call just to see a friendly face and maybe have a little chat. Angel always made time to chat, though it may mean her working later than she should.

She always remembered Billy telling her to be kind and to be generous with her time, that was so very important in life, he'd said. He was such a kind and gentle person, her dad, she would miss him forever.

Although not her biological father, there had always been a strong bond between them, her mother too. She'd never felt adopted, never had reason to feel like she didn't belong.

They were the best parents any child could ask for, she was so lucky to have them, or that they'd found her more like. Rose seemed in good spirits when she'd got home, had baked an apple tart and was mixing the cream when she walked into the kitchen.

It was good to see her smile, she needed it, it had been a tough day. Falling asleep on the sofa after the dinner and delicious apple tart for dessert, Angel had to give in and go to bed, her mother would follow when the movie had ended, she wasn't a fan of the bed since Billy had died.

Sleepless nights and flowing memories in the quiet of the night, not to mention the loneliness, was it any wonder she would sit watching anything on the TV until all hours to shorten the night.

Still giving her teddy Cleudo a snuggle as she got in to bed, Angel smiled to herself, maybe it was time to stop doing that. Even at twenty-two, it had brought her comfort, maybe soon, she'd thought but these nights, she needed a bit of comforting, still patching together the pieces of her broken heart.

Still feeling the pain of losing her dad, though waning a bit, she still had the pangs of loneliness. She needed her snuggles with Cleudo, who would have believed it! Katie had rang while she was out the next day, she was home for a week's holiday and wanted to meet up.

Angel was delighted to hear it, she hadn't seen her friend for so long, she would invite her over for tea, her mum would enjoy seeing her too and hearing about her travels. Full of the joys as usual, Katie came through the door like a hurricane, she had gifts for Rose and Angel.

Having not seen them since Billy had passed away, she spent the first hour of her visit sitting beside Rose on the sofa, talking about him and mostly listening to stories about him and how they'd missed him so much.

Rose was wound up, it was like she really needed to talk to someone and Katie was one of the best listeners she could have found. Angel busied herself in the kitchen once she'd found herself left out of the conversation, she'd winked at Katie in appreciation of her kind ways.

She'd held Rose's hand throughout the conversation and empathised with every word and every tear. "So, let's hear about your travels now, you must have loads of stories."

Rose sat back, more relaxed now with her cup of tea still in her hand, no doubt gone cold, Angel thought as she went to get the teapot from the kitchen to offer a hot drop to whoever wanted it. No takers, Angel sat down with a sigh.

In listening to Katie and her adventures, she wasn't sure if she envied her or maybe she was just tired but she felt a bit drained, she'd had a busy week, so she put it down to that. Why would she envy Katie, hadn't she been given the same opportunities herself and chosen to stay, she had no regrets whatsoever.

"Your mum looks well," sitting in the pub down the road, Katie had left the drinks on the table in front of Angel. Rose had told them to go and have a drink and a chat, she was going to have a bath and read a book.

There was no need to ask Katie twice, she was on her feet within seconds, thanking Rose for the hospitality and the lovely chat; she gave her a hug and promised to call by again before her holidays were over.

They chatted and laughed about their college days and joked about the boys they'd fallen in love with and the foolishness they'd got up to in those days. Angel felt revitalised as she watched Katie chat to a lad as she went to the bathroom.

A real looker, she was often chatted up when they were out, Angel remembered. It was nothing new, she was gone for a while before she returned with drinks.

Arguing with her as she'd got the last round of drinks, Katie informed her that the gentleman at the end of the bar had sent them over, had inquired as to what they were drinking when she passed him by on the way to the bathroom.

Looking round, Angel could see the familiar smile looking back at her; it was Frank, Jenny's visitor. He'd recognised her as he came in to the bar but Angel hadn't noticed him at all.

He wanted to thank her for her kindness to Jenny and Brod. "Way beyond your line of duty," he'd said as he stopped for a chat on his way out of the pub. He was driving, so he wasn't drinking, had just dropped in for a bit of company, he'd seemed very much alone, Angel thought.

She'd felt for him and thanked him for the drink and said it was very kind of him and there was no need. Jenny and Brod were just a pleasure to be around, she'd never thought of it as work, she actually looked forward to seeing them every time.

Katie went on to say she'd thought he was such a nice man and it would be a long time before any of her patients would complement her on her work. She'd gone on to do psychiatry specialising in mental health.

A very demanding career but so rewarding, she'd said. Angel could see her doing well in her field, she was so kind and caring, she hadn't discussed any of her patients but in speaking about her work as a whole, she could see she was devoted to it.

They arranged to meet up again at the same pub as it was convenient for all, Angel had wondered what that had meant but hadn't questioned it then.

She always hated to go into a pub on her own and Katie had remembered that, so they would meet outside and walk in together.

As they walked to the bar, they were greeted by half a dozen of their college mates, Katie had arranged it, thought it would be a nice way to end her holidays and a nice surprise for Angel.

Catching up on their mates and their news and their different paths in life was just what the doctor ordered, Angel was really enjoying the night, she didn't want it to end in fact. Shell or Shelly as was her right name, but they all called her Shell, had arrived late.

Sitting down after greeting them all with a hug and a kiss, she smiled as she introduced a man that had come from the bar and left a drink in front of her. "This is my cousin Eligh, he's home on holidays from Germany with his mum. I knew ye wouldn't mind him tagging along, he's been cooped up with the mothers all week."

Shell giggled as she went on to say he was probably going stir crazy. The night went fast and everybody seemed to enjoy themselves including Eligh. Though with a very German accent, he spoke good English, had sat beside Angel all night and was so interesting to talk to, she'd thought.

Once the bar had closed, they'd decided to go on to a night club, it had been a while since Angel had danced, she had argued that she was wearing the wrong shoes but Katie had dragged her onto the dance floor with the rest of them.

Eligh was surrounded by a pack of mad women, they'd had such a laugh. She would probably regret it in the morning but for now, she was enjoying herself and it had been a while. She'd rang Rose before they'd left the pub to tell her she would be late and not to wait up.

Rose was delighted to hear she was enjoying herself, she worked too hard, she thought it would do her good. They'd shared two taxis on the way home, had said their goodbye's to Katie and promised to all meet up again next time she was home.

Eligh would be on holidays for another three weeks, they'd come home for a month as he was on holidays from school and his mother hadn't seen her sister in years. It had been planned for a while and they would make it a long visit, his mother was getting on, so who'd know if they would make it home again.

He'd given it to her as a gift for her eightieth birthday. Eligh was the youngest of seven children, an afterthought his mother used to say with fifteen years between him and his next sibling.

A change of life baby, she'd say, none the worst for it, Angel thought to herself as she watched him speak on the way home in the taxi, he was a handsome man, a gentleman. None of that smartness usually seen in the men she had met in night clubs before, not that she would frequent them very often.

Indeed not at all in recent years but while in college, she would have gone out every week, usually on a Thursday night as was the case back then. Boys were pushy, forward, annoying, she'd often thought.

She'd just wanted to dance and enjoy the music back then but there'd always be a few pushing in on the dance floor where there'd be a few girls dancing. Eligh seemed old for his years, very sort of settled looking with his waistcoat and shirt and his black pants.

His hair was jet black, combed off his face with a little wave on the side, very attractive. With his German accent, even his speaking was attractive, had she passed him on the street, perhaps she might not have bat an eyelid.

She wasn't one to take notice but having been in his company all evening and him being such good company, she was wishing she might see more of him. As if to read her mind as they pulled up outside her house, Eligh jumped out from the front seat of the taxi and opened the door for her to get out, asking if maybe he might take her for something to eat sometime.

He had apologised for spending the ride home chatting to the taxi driver but she hadn't minded, she had spent the whole journey studying his profile. A strong jawline, of sallow complexion, his head almost hitting the roof of the car, he was tall.

As she stood motionless he awaited her reply with a polite grin on his face. Of course, they could go for something to eat, why not?

It would be her first real date in years; she'd met up with friends, both girls and boys in the past but not many on a one to one date. What were the chances? A guy comes to visit his relations from Germany and they end up going out.

Rose was delighted to hear Angel was stepping out (as she called it), it would do her good and it was about time. She spent too many hours on the road with her job, as much as she liked it, she needed other interests as well.

A young man was just what the doctor had ordered. Angel had to laugh, it was a meal out with a stranger, she informed her mother, sniggering, not a proposal. Wouldn't be buying a hat yet ma'am, she'd laughed.

"Well now, young lady, if you don't get a move on, I'll be walking you down the aisle on a frame. That's if I'll be able to walk at all," Rose replied and they both laughed.

Angel didn't want any fuss, so she had arranged to meet Eligh at the pub; after all, he was a stranger and probably wouldn't have a clue where to pick her up or where there was a decent place to eat.

The pub was nearby and had quite decent food for bar food, it would be fine. Eligh was waiting outside when she got there, she was bang on time, so he must have been early, she'd thought.

One never knows what's around the corner, what the next day could bring. One never knows! He looked quite handsome, she'd thought, standing there dressed very smart but casual.

As she crossed the road, he spotted her coming and began to make his way towards her, she hadn't noticed he'd walked with a limp the evening before, not that it mattered. In fact, she thought it was sort of attractive the way he walked.

The night went well, they chatted at ease and Angel had found him very interesting to talk to, he liked the outdoors, liked to mountain climb and had travelled around the world in doing it. A sport that had nearly put an end to his outdoor activities three years previous.

He'd travelled to India with the intention of climbing Mount Meru, a badly failed attempt. Apparently, he'd said it was reported as one of the hardest mountains to climb, which had made it all the more interesting to him.

He'd joined a team of climbers, looking up at the mountain, he went on to say it just looked like a big wall of granite straight up. It was irresistible, Angel could see the excitement in his face as he talked about it.

Failing to reach the peak, it had been on the descent that he'd lost his footing and fallen over two hundred feet, landing on a ledge below. Unconscious, he had been air lifted to hospital and remained in an induced coma for several days.

On awakening, he'd discovered he'd lost part of his leg, hence he walked with a limp. Lifting his trousers, he showed

Angel the price he had paid for his adventures. A prosthesis foot and knee had put an end to his climbing for now but not forever, he'd said, it would of course be harder but not impossible.

She'd expected she would hear of his interests and probably get to know him a bit better over dinner but this had left her in awe, though calm on the outside, she was traumatised inwardly.

The conversation had gotten a bit more relaxing as he had asked her about herself; her life journey so far had absolutely nothing of interest compared to his. But they chatted and laughed and chatted some more until it was time to go.

Chapter 4
Hypothermia

Rose had gone to bed when Angel got home, it was late and she'd had work in the morning. She'd had a lovely evening and had arranged to meet Eligh at the weekend for a drink, he was lovely company, though so far they didn't seem to have much in common but they'd got on well.

Climbing the stairs as quietly as she could, she passed her mother's room on her toes so as not to wake her. She wasn't surprised to hear her call out as she opened her own bedroom door.

She'd sat on the end of her mother's bed for as long as it took to go into every little detail of the evening, the questions were coming hot and heavy. Though late, Angel didn't feel at all tired; she'd felt sort of excited like the night before Christmas or the night before your birthday as a child when you can't sleep for the excitement.

Rose looked a bit pale, Angel thought as she looked at her across the breakfast table next morning, she wondered if maybe she wasn't feeling well. Not one to make a fuss, especially where she was concerned, Angel asked if everything was ok and she started to cry.

Not at all like Rose, Angel could feel her heart race in her chest, something must be wrong, she'd thought. Not one for running to the doctor's, she didn't think there was any point in suggesting it either.

Finally, it came to light that Rose had been having these feelings for a while; at that stage though, Angel had never noticed, she would all of a sudden break down and cry for no apparent reason.

Sure, she wasn't around to see these things happen, so taken up with her work, she had been spending less and less time at home with her mother and at the weekends, they would shop or maybe go for a spin if the day was nice on a Sunday.

She'd never noticed. In looking at her more closely, Angel could see that her mother looked tired and drawn as well. While she got up to pour the tea, Rose went on to say that her feelings were natural for her time of life, she was going through 'the change' as she called it.

Angel would have referred to it as the menopause. No wonder she was looking pale, she'd suffered it all on her own but not anymore.

Angel would be keeping an eye on her and ensure that she was getting proper nourishment to keep her strong throughout, it would be a long journey with many ups and downs but she would be there for her.

Though some women sailed through this time of life without a care, some would have it tough. Both mentally and physically. From feelings of dread to feelings of rage, from sweating from head to toe to bleeding with clots as big as your hand, wondering if maybe your womb had fallen through your cervix.

Angel had read about it all through her study years and already in her young life, she'd had feelings of dread about it but she would have to deal with it like every other woman in the world.

There was no doubt in her mind but that it was a man's world, no doubt at all. Rose seemed happy to have shared her feelings with her daughter, assuring her that there were days when she was absolutely fine too but those days were becoming fewer and fewer as time was going on.

Sometimes, she'd said she'd felt like her heart was going to jump out of her chest, she was losing her confidence in going out of late on account of not knowing when these feelings would hit.

There would be no warning, one minute she would be fine, out and about doing a bit of shopping or whatever, next minute she would feel like she was going to pass out and panic.

Life's journey into old age, though Rose was only in her early sixties, was like a rollercoaster of emotions but nature would have to take its own course. We just have to plod along and go with the flow, she'd said with a look of fear on her face.

Knowing there were medications that made the transition a little easier, Angel offered to take her to her doctor for a chat but as she'd expected, Rose would leave it with Mother Nature and that was the end of that; no point in arguing with her, she wouldn't be persuaded.

Angel would see to it that she got plenty of iron in her diet and might get her to take a natural supplement. Concern for her mother had overtaken the excitement of meeting Eligh at the weekend, she'd been so looking forward to it but now she didn't like leaving Rose on her own.

However, if she cancelled, Rose would be cross; she'd know exactly what she was thinking about, she was so good at that. Doing her best to be upbeat, Rose had asked Angel to leave her outfit that she planned to wear out on her bed and she would iron it for her.

Angel hadn't mentioned going out but obviously, her mother had remembered her saying it on the night she'd chatted to her on the bed after being out with Eligh. She would have to go along with it and look interested even though all she'd felt was worry.

She thanked her mother and told her she was an angel, gave her a hug and was off on her travels to look after her patients.

She so loved her job but today, she'd felt a dark cloud hanging over her; she couldn't wait to get home to see that Rose was ok. Her outfit ironed to perfection and left on her bed, she'd smiled to herself.

"Am I spoilt or what?" Rose was having a snooze on the chair, so she thought she wouldn't disturb her. Rose would have eaten earlier, knowing that Angel would be eating out, though the smell of bacon and turnip was so good, Angel would have settled for that.

All showered and spruced up, the worries of the day washed away, she sat on her bed with her jewellery box on her lap. Going through her earrings mostly costume, she thought to herself, "Nothing worth robbing here," though they were only cheap, they were pretty and she liked to match her earrings with what she was wearing.

She felt good the best she had felt in a long time, but there was a little niggle at the back of her mind still, she didn't feel right leaving Rose on her own, it was early days after losing Billy and she was struggling with her time of life.

She would tell Eligh that she'd enjoyed the night and make her excuses for next time, she wanted to be with her mother any chance she'd get and she'd felt selfish putting herself first.

Anyway, it wouldn't go anywhere, sure how could it with thousands of miles between them, she wasn't into holiday flings. Eligh was a lovely guy and she wished him well and hoped to stay friends, he'd promised to keep in touch and they exchanged addresses.

The timing was off that was all, who knows had they met under different circumstances, things might be different, there was definitely a spark there. Rose was disappointed to hear they wouldn't be meeting again. Angel seemed so happy when she spoke about him.

There was no need to explain, her mother would go mad if she knew how Angel had felt about leaving her to go out. In time, when Rose was a bit stronger, there would be plenty of time for herself.

It was a difficult time and Angel needed her mother's company as much as she needed hers right now. When Angel called on Jenny and Brod next day, they seemed busy, Jenny had a box of old photos on her bed and they were looking through them.

The tea was made and Jenny was going through the photos, showing Angel her most treasured memories of days long gone. The children were young in most of them, looked like it had been a very busy house at one time.

The garden manicured to perfection by Brod, a wonderful gardener, Jenny said. There were photos of neighbours and neighbours' children all gathered at one time or another, mostly on sunny days.

"Look," Jenny sat up straight in the bed, "Frank was hoping I might come across some of these." Frank as a young boy was photographed with a dog in their back garden, there was another little boy with him, she'd said he was his brother who had died very young.

Her face changed as she went deep into thought, she talked about the tragedy that his death had brought about.

Brod looked on with concern on his face, obviously this family meant a lot to both of them. She would give the photos to Frank when he called again. Angel had enjoyed the walk down memory lane with them, seems they used to do it on a regular basis until the tragedy occurred.

Not going into much detail, Angel just went along with it and didn't ask, not wanting to seem nosey. As she reached the bottom of the box, Jenny took out a little teddy bear.

"This is Cleudo," explaining how she came to have him, she went on to say that he was all she had left of the lovely family that had lived next door all those years ago, she'd said it seemed like another lifetime.

Driving home, Angel felt a bit unsettled, it was strange how she had a teddy called Cleudo as well, it all seemed a bit eerie or something, she'd thought, she didn't know why. One thing she did know was that Jenny wasn't parting with Cleudo, not ever.

Her day had been as ordinary as any other day, so she didn't know why she was feeling like this. A nice long bath when she got home, that would do the job, she'd thought. It was forecast to be the coldest night on record with ice and snow with northerly winds.

She would snuggle up in front of the fire and chat with Rose, maybe open a bottle of wine. Throughout the night, Jenny and Brod came into her thoughts a few times, something wasn't right, if she didn't know better, she'd have said they were clearing out.

Brod had been burning papers in the stove and he had seemed a bit sad or something. She hoped all would be back to normal on her next visit. Just down the road from where Brod and Jenny lived, Angel had to call on one of her older patients.

Phyllis had a bedridden brother Tom that she cared for, always with a story. Angel enjoyed her visits. Half the times she took what she'd said with a pinch of salt. Tom used to say she'd spent her day at the curtain in case a cat might pass by and she'd miss it, Angel would laugh.

She would call in on Brod and Jenny afterwards although it wasn't her day to visit and it was more for her own peace of mind if she was honest. As she was about to ring the bell, the door opened and Phyllis was standing there.

She looked in shock, Angel was expecting the worst and thought something had happened to Tom. "Awful business down the road." Angel listened while she went on to say the nice couple down the road had been found dead.

Angel's heart sank, she felt numb. She apologised to Phyllis and went back out to the car. Turning the corner, she could see the commotion outside the house, Jenny and Brod's house.

Stopped at the gate by the guard, she explained how Jenny was a patient of hers and he let her through. Walking through the front door, her heart was racing, there was no one to be seen. Then she heard the voices coming from the back door.

"Hypothermia," the doctor was talking to the guard at the back door. "So sad," he'd said.

Angel couldn't see past them and couldn't make out what they were talking about. On the garden seat with their arms wrapped around each other sat Jenny and Brod, death having stolen the colour from their faces, they looked grey.

Icicles forming on their grey hair, though an air of silence prevailed, there was also peace. Angel wasn't allowed to go too near as much as she longed to throw her arms around them and maybe warm them, maybe bring them back to life although long gone.

The report had stated that they had been dead for hours. The coldest of nights on record, why would they sit lightly clad. They had a plan and Angel should have read the signs, she knew things weren't as normal the day before, she just knew it.

Their family notified, they were coming from all corners of the world to find their beautiful parents like this. Their limbs would have to be broken to lay them to rest, she overheard the doctor say as they had frozen in a sitting position.

As Jenny's nurse, Angel would offer her assistance in any way it would be needed in the coming days. Heartbroken, she offered her help, what else could she do, they weren't to know that Jenny had become more than a patient and Brod as well, they had become good friends and Angel was feeling the hurt as much as any family member.

She felt sick to her stomach. It was arranged that she would call back there in the afternoon when by which time, it was hoped they would have a clearer picture. The doctor didn't see any delays likely as there had been a note found in Jenny's hand. It had been a planned suicide.

Angel couldn't stop shaking, the car seemed miles away although just outside the gate, she'd felt like she was walking over hills. The ground was coming up to meet her, the shock of it all had almost taken her breath away, let alone her walk.

Glad to reach the car door without falling down, she held on to the steering wheel with the tightest grip, she would have to wait a while to overcome her weakness. She was in no fit state to drive, not yet!

As the shock subsided, she watched as the house she knew so well as a quiet and welcoming home became a crime scene. Two lovely people she came to know and love, now victims of what seemed like a planned event to end their life together. How long had they been planning this?

Angel was daunted by the scenes, how she would face this in the afternoon. She drove home in bewilderment, probably not fit to drive but no one was aware of the closeness she'd felt for them, so why would they worry that she would be in shock.

Only just making it to the bathroom, she left what had only been in her stomach a couple of hours in the bathroom sink. Rose had been making her bed when she heard the crying, not able to understand what she was saying for the tears, she just held her daughter until she had cried enough.

She was pale as death and still shivering as she spoke, now a little more calm and composed. Rose had never seen anyone so upset, it sounded like a shocking sight, it was no wonder that the poor girl was in shock.

Nothing could prepare one for that. Awakening after getting her head down for a couple of hours, Angel had a ferocious headache, her head was pounding. She was due to go to Jenny and Brod's house within the hour, so she would have to take a pain killer and get on with it.

Now looking more or less back to normal apart from a guard standing in the doorway, she assumed the bodies had been moved, she dreaded the thought of going into the house. Going up to the guard, she explained her being there only to be told the bodies had been removed to the funeral parlour under the instructions of the family.

The scene had been cordoned off and the house would be locked up until the family had arrived. Angel was so relieved, she wasn't able to face it again, her stomach was still churning. Obviously, she would be available to help in any way that she could in the days to come, she left her details with the guard and went off.

It was a nightmare, there would be no sleep, it would be a long night. She thought of Jenny and Brod, went over and over her chat with them the previous day in the hope that something would spring to mind as to their plans. But there was nothing apart from what seemed like a clear out going on that day, she wouldn't have questioned that.

That would be something anyone would do at any time. Checking in at work, she arranged to have a few days off, understandably her boss had said she wouldn't be in a fit state after such a tragedy as she had witnessed.

She was offered counselling and as much time as she needed, getting cover wasn't a problem. Never having met their children, Angel was surprised to hear from Jenny and

Brod's daughter later that week, she hadn't been sleeping and had just dropped off on the chair when the phone rang.

Sounded like a lovely person, Angel thought to herself, the apple doesn't fall far from the tree. They chatted for a while and Erica filled her in on the funeral arrangements, adding that she would very much like for her to be there when her parents were brought home that evening.

They would wake them in the house and they would go to the chapel the following day. With burial in the churchyard after the mass. Of course she would be there, she was so happy to be invited.

Seeing Jenny and Brod again might even help her to come to terms with it all. She hadn't been doing so well on her own so far, even questioning if perhaps she was in the wrong job!

There was so much heartbreak on a daily basis, people struggling in living on their own, sleeping in their own excrement in not being able to get to the bathroom at night for fear of falling.

Even just the lonesome look in their eyes on losing their life long partner and having no choice but to live alone. But then there was the very fulfilling side of it, in meeting such wonderful people every day, so happy to see you be it to get help in changing their bedsheets or just to sit and chat for a while after changing a dressing.

Very simple things, all very basic needs but to someone living alone, these simple tasks were like a mountain to climb every single day. She wasn't sure she was strong enough after witnessing such a tragedy with Jenny and Brod, so much in love that they couldn't bear to leave one another behind.

To leave one alone to face the world, they had decided for themselves rather to go together, in the most simplest of ways.

Had they suffered? She didn't know but she did know that they would have shivered, hence their wrapping around each other when discovered.

Their organs would have failed as a result of the cold and would have become unconscious, after which death wouldn't be far off. She would forever wonder why, what sort of love was so strong that it could destroy life itself, was the fear of being left behind to live alone so frightening?

She would have to get out of the car and walk to the door, whether her legs could carry her or not was the question, they felt like jelly. Erica had said it would be nice if she was there before the hearse had arrived, just for support.

The girls were devastated, asking why and how their parents had seemed that day that Angel had visited last, she wasn't able to shine any light on the reason why, only to say they had been in great form the previous day, looking at old photos and reminiscing.

She had enjoyed her time with them as she always did, they were like old friends to her. She would miss them dreadfully, she told them.

As they carried the two coffins up the path, the neighbours lined each side of the pathway while their family hardly able to stand, stood at the door, Angel stood with the neighbours as was her place, she'd thought.

Unable to hold back the tears, she could feel her body shake with grief as the two coffins carried by their twelve grandchildren, some only tall enough to reach the others shoulder, passed by her.

It was the saddest thing she had ever seen. The younger grandchildren sobbing as they walked, the older ones more composed, though heartbreak evident on their faces. Pictures of their wedding day and of many different occasions placed on each coffin as the lids remained closed, requested by the family as it was too much to bear.

Having had time at the funeral parlour to view the remains of their lovely mother and father and say their goodbyes, they'd decided that they couldn't take any more. It was all they could do to keep breathing, holding on to each other, they approached the coffins and cried their fill.

Tears dropping onto the lid of each coffin were unbearable to watch, cries from their broken hearts inconsolable. How they were ever going to carry on after such a calamity, Angel would question.

There were prayers and tea and chatting and memories, each neighbour donated their own memories of a couple loved by all and thought of as generous and kind. Angel left with a heavy heart, no healing done.

If anything, she'd felt worse, there was this awful guilt that she'd felt since that awful day, why hadn't she seen this coming. Does one ever know what's going on in another person's mind at any one time?

As she got into the car, Noreen, the eldest of the girls called to her, there had been a little box left in Jenny's bedroom with a note, asking that it should be given to their dear nurse Angel.

Taking the box tied with a red ribbon, Angel could feel a lump in her throat, Noreen wished her well and thanked her for the care she had taken of her mother. It was obvious that she had meant a lot to both her mother and father, they had often spoken about her when they'd call on the phone.

At that stage, she squeezed Angel's hand and started to choke on her words. Angel put the box on the back seat of the car, knowing it would be a while before she would be able to face looking into it. A good while! The funeral was beautiful, if a funeral could ever be called beautiful, but it reflected a loving family bound together with loving parents, a childhood of happy memories had by them all.

Tormented with grief, yet Jenny and Brod's family had done them proud. Although invited back to the house after the burial, Angel choose not to go, apart from being exhausted with the events of the past few days, she didn't feel she could be of any support to them.

She wasn't in a good place, she would go home. Rose was cooking an apple tart, Angel's favourite. She knew she was struggling these past few days, so she thought she would spoil her. They sat and talked until Angel gave in to sleep, Rose took the blanket from the sofa and gently threw it over her, her heart was broken for her daughter.

Having slept for a few hours, Angel woke with a crick in her neck, but at least she had slept and felt the better for it. She would shower and freshen up and maybe take her mum to her dad's grave, she'd been thinking about him all day and needed to visit the grave.

Rose was delighted to go, she too missed Billy with all her heart, she was still just putting one foot in front of the other every day. Standing at her father's grave, she could no longer hold back the tears, she cried for her dad, for her dear friends Jenny and Brod, and she cried for the days to come.

She wasn't sure if she could face the days to come, she felt broken, she would have to take some time off, perhaps even have some counselling as was suggested by her boss. Taking away the withered flowers from her dad's grave, she would put them into the bag she had taken the fresh ones out of and leave them on the back seat of the car to dump when she got home.

The boot was full of stuff from the clinic and she didn't want to risk any dirt getting on them, they were sterile and needed to be kept in a clean place. Leaving the bag on the back seat, she spotted the box that Noreen had given her, her mother looking on, asked her what the box was.

Angel explained to Rose that Jenny and Brod had wished her to have it. "Not today," she had said to her mother and sat into the driving seat, her hands physically shaking and she took her keys out of her pocket.

Rose put her hand on her daughter's hand as if to say, 'it will be ok', but no words were said. Sometimes, silence can speak louder than words! Angel took the box to her bedroom and left it in the drawer beside her bed, she would open it in due course when she felt a bit stronger, she did wonder what could be inside.

Rose had the kettle on within minutes, she was standing at the back door when Angel came down from upstairs. She knew by looking at her mother that Mother Nature had struck again, she'd felt hot and panicky and went to the back door for air, she was finding her menopause hard.

"A roller coaster of emotions," she had said in talking about it recently. Angel had been so wrapped up in her own feelings in the last week or more that she hadn't even asked her mother how she was feeling.

Today, the fear and anxiety were evident in her face, she wasn't the confident person she used to be since this new era of her life had hit, and hit so hard. But at least they were talking about it now and talking helps, talking always helps.

There wasn't much Angel could do for her, only to be there to support her, she wouldn't hear of getting a doctor involved, it was natural and "what's natural isn't always wonderful," she would say and laugh.

Angel couldn't get the picture of Jenny and Brod out of her mind, especially when she'd go to bed at night, it would haunt her. Her dreams were of weird things, she would wake up in a sweat and sometimes fail to get back to sleep at all.

Hence, she was constantly tired, she would go for a nice walk and clear her head, she thought as she got up out of bed, exhausted as usual. It had been three weeks since that awful day and she would soon have to consider returning to work again, though the thought of it alone sent her into panic mode.

How would she cope in passing Jenny and Brod's house every day, and she would have to as it was on her route. As she walked round the park, she began to feel calm and more relaxed, the walk was doing her good.

It would have been good for her mother to walk as well but she had said no when she had asked her to go with her. She'd been flooding all night and was afraid to be too far from the toilet.

Angel thought maybe she would get her an iron supplement to take, she must be lacking in iron in losing all of that blood. That would explain her tiredness and anxiousness as well, she might even take one herself!

In talking to the pharmacist as she called in to the chemist on her way home, the lady advised that she really should be checked out by her doctor but recommended the iron supplement and said it would do no harm.

There was no chance of her going to the doctor but Angel hoped she might take the supplement. As she opened the door of the chemist on the way out, she noticed Mrs Mc Dee's son crossing the road, it wasn't a nice thing to do but she wasn't up to talking yet and she knew he would be asking how she was and probably when she would be back on her route again.

Mrs Mc Dee was one of her lovely old ladies on her route every day and she should have asked him how she was but she decided to hide behind one of the shelves until he had passed by. He might even bring up the tragedy that was Jenny and Brod, she just wasn't up to talking to people yet.

Chapter 5
The Box

Rose was in the garden when she returned from her walk, seemed cheerful and happy to be pottering around. They chatted for a few minutes and Angel said she was going for a shower, she had agreed to take the iron supplement.

"Sure, whatever good it might do, it won't do me any harm," Rose had said. As she opened the drawer beside her bed to leave her watch in her jewellery box, inside she saw the box that Jenny had left for her.

Would she be strong enough to open it? She would see, maybe after her shower. As she shakily took it in her hand, a wave of loneliness came over her, she'd opened the red ribbon gently, knowing it had been tied with love.

The box had a note inside and a letter in an envelope and a little teddy, the teddy she always had beside her bed when she had called on her. She read the note, barely able to see the words for the tears blinding her.

Jenny had explained that the box had been tied with a ribbon that had belonged to a very special little girl that she had known and loved and the teddy too. The letter was from Frank, the man that had visited her and used to send her flowers, a man that lived next door to Jenny and Brod a long time ago.

Going on to say that the letter had confirmed her suspicions, Jenny wrote that she hoped Angel would read it and take it from there and wished her luck and a happy life. She hoped that their decision to end their lives together wouldn't upset her too much and she wasn't to feel in any way responsible though she was the last one to speak to them the day before.

She couldn't have known, they had kept things as normal as they could, so that they wouldn't be suspected and ruin their plan. It had always been their plan to go together, it was only a matter of picking the right moment.

Living without each other, whoever had gone first would have been too hard, they would be happy now and no one could take that away.

Totally confused by the note, Angel proceeded to open the letter addressed to Jenny. Why would she want her to read a letter from Frank, a man she hardly knew, that was addressed to Jenny.

Her hair was dripping wet down her back after the shower but she hardly noticed, she was bewildered, nothing was making sense and as she read Frank's letter, she was even more so.

It read how he had received a letter in the post that was on the floor behind his front door when he'd returned from Moira's funeral all those years ago. Angel was still more confused, who was Moira?

In speaking to Jenny on his last visit, he knew she'd had suspicions about the tragedy that was. Moira had explained how she was finding life unbearable and had decided to end her misery, she had thought that she was unfit to look after a baby and wanted her child to have a better chance in life other than a mother that was so lost after the death of her husband, that she was beginning to resent the child.

If he had received the letter, the deed had been done, she wanted him to find their baby girl that she had left on the steps of a social services office. But she hadn't said where, Frank had enquired in every corner of the country to no avail.

He'd always had suspicions about Olivia after he was told about her, he'd had a short affair with Moira and putting two and two together and the fact that his brother and Moira had such difficulty conceiving up to then put him thinking.

He wasn't about to burst their bubble and God knows, maybe break up their marriage over a silly and short lived affair. Obviously, Moira felt the same. But he always had his suspicions.

He hadn't mentioned the letter from Moira to anyone until Jenny had talked about Moira on his last visit to see her, how she had said to Brod that she would never have brought the baby with her, whatever about doing away with herself and she must have been in an awful way to have done that, she wouldn't have done that to dear little Olivia.

When he'd returned home having had what Jenny said going around in his head the whole way home, he decided he would tell her about the letter from Moira. Showing the letter to Brod, she had said, "I knew it. I knew it."

However, her suspicions had gone further, though she hadn't mentioned it to Frank or indeed not even to Brod, she had kept it to herself but as time had gone on, her suspicions had gotten stronger and stronger!

She could feel it in her heart and she was seldom wrong when it came to the affairs of the heart. Having read Frank's letter, she was convinced, though not called Olivia now, Angel had all of her mother's traits as well as looks and from day one when she visited Jenny first, she could feel the connection, her heart had raced when she saw her.

It could have been Moira standing there, same kind ways, same smile, there was something special about this girl, there was no doubt. Having gotten to know her over time and discovering she had been adopted as a baby had convinced Jenny that she was right.

None the wiser, Angel left the box on the bed and continued to dry her hair, her mother peeped into her bedroom to tell her the lunch was ready.

Noticing the box on the bed, she'd asked if there was anything nice in the box. Angel read the letter to her mother and while folding it, after she noticed the writing on the back of the letter, she hadn't noticed it before and it was in different handwriting than the actual letter, more than likely Jenny's, she'd thought.

It wrote "Frank's phone number." Rose had a sinking feeling now, after all those years could it be that her darling Angel's family had come looking for her. She felt a lump in her throat and had to rush to the bathroom, it was like any feeling of emotion nowadays brought on a feeling of panic, her heart was racing.

She wondered if she would see the other side of this menopause and its horrendous symptoms, it was killing her. She ran the cold tap on the back of her wrist, a tip her mother had told her that helped with the overwhelming feeling of a hot flush.

Angel had gone downstairs when she came out of the bathroom, thinking her mother looked very pale, she asked her if she was ok. Smiling, Rose continued on into the kitchen, not knowing what to think, where would this letter lead her daughter though not having given birth to her, apart from that, she was every bit her daughter and she the only mother her daughter had ever known.

This letter could change everything now. Angel too knew on reading it again that it could only mean one thing, but how did Jenny make that connection? Had she said anything to Frank, did he even know that Angel saw the letter he had sent to Jenny in confidence?

This was indeed a puzzle. If this was as it sounded, the man that had died all those years ago, the husband of her birth mother who had taken her own life and drowned, wasn't in fact her father; Frank that she had met and admired as being a very mannerly man, kind and very respectful towards her would be her father!

Thinking back, she remembered thinking to herself that she'd felt she'd known him before, he was so easy to talk to, it had just felt right somehow. It was a strange feeling, it had been a strange few weeks in fact, where would she go from here?

What did Jenny want her to do and what did she mean when she said to take it from there! Rose had said nothing right through the lunch, usually so chatty, Angel felt she had to say something, she had been told at a very young age that she had been adopted but had never thought of her birth parents until now, she had a very happy childhood and had no reason to look into her past.

They had chatted for quite some time, both airing their own particular views on the matter with Rose also airing her fears. To which Angel very quickly put her mind at ease, whatever came out of this letter would have no bearing on their relationship none whatsoever, as far as she was concerned, Rose was and always would be her mother and in fact, her very best friend.

Whether it was because she had been adopted or maybe they'd had a bond from her childhood but Angel was very close to her mother, she'd always known she could talk to her about anything and confide in her if she'd had any fears.

A huge advantage in growing up, she knew now, in talking to parents; sometimes on her rounds, having difficulties with teenagers and not being able to talk to their growing children, she had many times thanked her lucky stars that she had been blessed with both her mother and father in having such a good relationship with them.

Nothing would change there and anyway, she'd told her mother she wasn't even sure she would pursue the matter any further, she would have to think about it. Lying in bed that night, she'd taken the letter out again to read, would she ring Frank?

He'd apologised for not being able to attend the funeral of his dear friends and neighbours. Erica, Jenny and Brod's youngest daughter, had said when they'd arrived home that she had contacted Frank as soon as she'd heard the awful news herself.

He'd broken down and hung up the phone, taking a good while to ring her back. He would visit in his own time but for now, he wouldn't be able to face such a tragedy, he had apologised and Erica had told him that she fully understood, it was a hard thing to face, she was struggling with it herself.

She'd added that he'd had bad memories from the past when he'd lost his only brother so suddenly, to be followed by the tragedy of his brother's wife drowning. Oblivious at the time that Erica had been talking about her birth mother, Angel had felt for Frank even as a stranger listening to his story.

Life could be so cruel. Looking at Rose and remembering all the chats they'd had with Billy of course as well, about the joy they'd felt when they had got the news that the adoption had gone through.

Angel recalled the day she had been told she was adopted, she remembered it being a strange feeling she didn't really understand, things didn't really feel any different afterwards though she remembered thinking they might.

Over the years that feeling had just faded into the background of her life, and losing her dad, her adoptive dad had hurt like hell just as if he had been her biological father she'd imagined.

The same feeling of loss, the same love stolen from her life, he had been her dad in every sense of the word. Being adopted was a beautiful way to live your life, had she been brought up by her biological parents, probably would have been wonderful too but she would never know now.

Angel truly believed one's path in life was laid out for them, she was one of the lucky ones. It had been three weeks now since she had experienced the tragedy that was Jenny and Brod, it was time she had thought about returning to work.

Hard as it would be, her boss had been very considerate in allowing her this much time to come to terms with it. In speaking to her on the phone, her boss had asked if she was sure that she was ready to return; it would be a bit raw yet, she had said.

Suggesting she take a desk job for a while, she mentioned that the clinic were run off their feet and were considering taking on a clinic nurse to organise appointments and such for home visits.

Angel had thought about it for a while and realised it was probably the best thing to do under the circumstances. She remembered she had avoided Mrs Mc Dee's son the week before, not wanting to talk about Jenny and Brod.

She would have to face a lot more heartache in going back on her rounds, it was the right thing to do for now. Maybe down the road a bit, she would be stronger to face it all, her boss had said.

It was going to be strange working at a desk, she had taken on this job initially because of her love of people, especially the elderly. It was so satisfying to see a face light up to see you coming, to be able to bring a bit of ease to someone suffering the pain of a wound after surgery when she would change the dressing.

Small simple things be it a little chat after attending a patient with loneliness written all over their faces. These were the things that made her job so worthwhile, ordinary everyday chores that become like mountains to climb to an elderly person living on their own, hardly able to climb the stairs with the pain of an ulcerated leg, never mind to fill the bucket with coal.

She'd organised many of her patients to receive home help when they didn't even know it was available to them.

Old and out of touch, they would struggle on with every bit of strength in their bodies.

It would be such a pleasure to see them getting the help they were entitled to. Working at a desk may have its rewards as well, she'd thought in driving towards the clinic, she would have to give it a fair chance and see how it would go. Parking outside the front of the clinic, she wondered if she was taking someone else's place.

'Staff' was written on the wall above, so she hoped it would be ok. Her boss was there to greet her, she hadn't seen her face to face since the tragedy of Jenny and Brod. She was very empathetic towards her and made her feel very welcome, offered her a cup of tea and introduced her to the other three girls in the office. Angel would have dealt with one or two of them over the phone, she was sure but had never met them in person.

In sitting at her desk, she felt out of place, as nice as everyone had been in welcoming her, she wasn't at all sure about working at a desk, perhaps she would settle in after a while. Full training was given and after a few weeks, she was left to deal with the phone queries on her own.

Rose could see that Angel wasn't happy, she had lost her spark, she would come home after her day and just go about quietly like as if she was constantly thinking about something. She had asked her on several occasions how her day had went but it would always be a short answer like 'Fine' or 'Ok'.

She had always liked to talk about her day. Rose knew she was missing her patients, being on the road and helping people. After all that was why she had trained in nursing in the first place, her love of people, her caring ways, she was sure a desk job wasn't what she wanted and it wouldn't take too long before she would pack it in but she wasn't going to say anything.

Angel would come to her when she was ready, she was sure of that, she just hadn't decided yet. It didn't take long, she'd come home one evening after being in the job no more than a couple of months and started to cry.

Rose had been taking a roast out of the oven and when she turned round in the kitchen, Angel was standing at the table, sobbing. After a nice cup of tea and a chat, all was revealed, a desk job wasn't for her, she would give her notice next day and take a bit of time, she wasn't yet ready to go back on her route nursing as much as she missed it; she wondered if maybe she would ever be ready.

Her head was all over the place and she felt she'd had too much time to think in sitting at a desk, she'd found herself constantly thinking about Jenny's letter and Frank and everything else that went with it, it was driving her crazy!

Rose pitied her, it was evident in her face that she was all over the place, trying to keep a face on for everyone and inside falling to pieces, she was only glad that she had come to her. A bit of time to herself and a good rest would do her good, she was looking tired, maybe she should look into that letter that Jenny had left for her, maybe she needed to.

She had left it in the drawer alright, she'd told her that but she was carrying it around in her head, it was eating away at her. Rose asked her to maybe think about getting in touch with Frank; after all, Jenny had given her his number, maybe she had sent a letter to Frank as well, maybe he was waiting for her to get in touch.

Angel's face changed and her eyes lit up, she hugged her mother and assured her again that it would make no difference to their relationship whatsoever. She had wanted to contact Frank lately, she'd felt she'd let Jenny down and it was getting her down but she didn't want to upset Rose.

Her boss was very understanding when she gave her notice, she offered to keep her job for her for as long as it took, she didn't want to lose her, she was a good nurse. Angel had thanked her but had said that she couldn't ask her to do that, she wasn't sure when she might be ready if ever.

They parted on good terms and she felt such relief, it was like a load had been lifted, a load she could no longer carry. She went to the graveyard to tell Billy, she would often stroll in there and have a chat with him, she was sure he was listening, it was a sort of calm feeling.

She felt better as she walked towards the gate. As the man approached her, she thought she recognised him, the sun was shining right into her eyes so that it was impossible to see right anyway, it was the time of day when the sun was blinding.

"Angel." Looking up, she had to shade her eyes, she hated the sun in her eyes, it always gave her a migraine, why didn't she bring her glasses out of the car.

It was Frank, for a moment she hesitated! Where had he come from? Seems he was in town on business and took the opportunity to visit Jenny and Brod at their resting place. Awful tragedy, he had said.

Angel hadn't gone to their grave that day though they were buried not far from Billy, she just wasn't in the form, she had gone there to talk to her dad. Frank wasn't sure where they were buried but Jenny's daughter had told him the graveyard and given him instructions, he hadn't been doing very well in following them but he wouldn't give up.

It had been his third time round the graveyard, he had said laughing, said he needed the exercise anyway. Angel turned back and brought him to where his very dear friends lay, the flowers now withered, she wondered who would look after the grave, as far as she knew, all of Jenny and Brod's family were away.

She would keep an eye on it, there wouldn't be a problem, she would be there anyway to see her dad. She and Frank cleared the old flowers into the skip by the gate and Frank lay his beautiful bouquet of flowers on the grave, kissing the ribbon as he lay them there.

Angel felt for him, he seemed very fond of the folks, any time she saw him with them, one would be forgiven to think that he was one of their own! They had chatted away while tending the grave, Frank had laid a beautiful bouquet on the grave and had a second bouquet of flowers left at the side of the grave, obviously he intended visiting another grave in the graveyard.

As Angel got up to go, he'd picked up the second bouquet and told her he had someone else to say hello to while he was there. His brother and his sister-in-law. Angel had felt sick, Frank hadn't mentioned the letter, so she assumed Jenny hadn't written to him regarding her suspicion.

She'd stumbled as she rose to her feet and Frank had caught her, asking if she was ok, she assured him she was fine and that she'd fallen out of her shoe. This was so awkward, she wanted to talk to him and she had agreed with Rose that she would contact him but she wasn't prepared to walk into him in the cemetery.

Would she ask him to join her for a coffee perhaps or would that be a strange thing to do? As though reading her mind, Frank invited her to walk with him to his brother and sister-in-law's grave and maybe, they could have a coffee after.

He was in town for a couple of days and was at a loose end, the work had been sorted at that stage and he was taking a couple of days to chill. He said he would love to chat about Jenny and Brod, Angel took a very deep breath and agreed to walk with him.

Her legs like jelly as she approached the grave, just like Jenny and Brod's grave, it was a bit neglected but then there was nobody around to keep an eye on it, well not until then!

She'd felt a sort of peace as she stood there and all of a sudden, out of the blue, she had started to well up, there was definitely something about this place, a connection of some sort.

As Frank stood at the counter of the café, Angel was rehearsing what she might say to bring about the dreaded discussion, she was terrified but she needn't have worried. Frank had started the conversation about his dear friends Jenny and Brod and one thing had led to another.

They talked for a good while, he spoke about his childhood living next door to them and how they were like family to himself and his brother Tom! This was her cue, it couldn't be easier, Jenny had asked her to take it from there, she had to do something.

Taking the letter out of her bag where she had carried it for over a week, thinking of dialling the number on the back, she had built herself up so much that her hand was shaking. Frank excused himself and went to the men's room. Deep breaths, she'd told herself, deep breaths!

When Frank came back to the table, Angel had left the letter in front of his coffee, now gone cold they had chatted so much. Looking at her in confusion, she smiled and asked him to read it, recognising the writing, he looked more confused than ever. Had she opened a can of worms?

It was done now and there was no going back, as she went into detail of how Jenny had suspicions from the first time they'd met, which for her were confirmed on hearing she had been adopted as a baby.

Frank looked into her eyes and for a while, he didn't say anything, taking the letter again in his hand, he'd said, "Oh my God, oh my God!"

Angel wasn't sure if that was a good reaction or what or maybe just shock, Frank was definitely in shock; what was she thinking, it was an awful thing to pounce on someone, she had felt the same after reading the letter the first time herself.

He apologised and took hold of her hand across the table. "I have looked for you, oh my God, for so long. I…I—" He started to cry and Angel didn't know where to look. She hardly knew this man and now all of a sudden, they were related.

This wasn't the place to talk, Angel thought maybe she would invite him to dinner and introduce him to Rose, they could talk then. Rose was so happy when she heard what had happened until panic took over.

"What would she do for dinner?" She had planned a shepherd's pie but that wouldn't do now, she would have to go to the butchers and get a nice bit of roast, this was indeed a special occasion.

As she busied round the kitchen, Angel took out the hoover and spruced up the cushions on the sofa, she felt both excited and afraid. She wished Billy was there, he would bring calm to any situation.

Rose had dinner organised in no time and the kitchen smelled of roast beef with all the trimmings, all that was to do now was to make the gravy. She would use the juices of the meat that would be nice, she'd thought, she couldn't remember when she'd felt this excited to have someone to dinner; in fact, she couldn't remember when she had last had someone to dinner, let alone a complete stranger.

But if he was of Angel's blood, he would have to be nice, it would be grand. Angel was wondering what she would wear, her favourite colour was green, probably because Billy had once told her the colour green brought out the green in her eyes, she would argue that her eyes were blue but he would insist that there was a hint of green in them as well.

She did miss Billy. Eight o clock on the dot, the doorbell rang. Frank stood there, holding a bunch of roses as she greeted him with a nervous smile, it was a strange situation.

"I think the florist down the road thinks she has competition, this is my third bouquet of flowers from them today. She probably thinks I'm setting up shop."

Angel took the flowers and thanked him and as they walked into the kitchen, she introduced him to Rose who wiped her hands in her apron before she shook his. He had a very strong grip, she'd told Angel later, he had squeezed her hand with a tear in his eyes.

He'd thanked her with such a sincere look on his face that she knew right away it was to do with giving Angel such a lovely home and upbringing. He was the perfect gentleman but then Angel already knew that, in watching him when he visited Jenny and Brod, you could tell he was the sincere type; she had admired that in him before.

Dinner went off well and after they had sat at the table for hours talking, and crying and talking and crying some more. Now she knew the whole story, Tom, Frank's brother had died suddenly, leaving Moira heartbroken, so much so that she couldn't go on.

She had written to Frank the day before she had decided to take her own life and leave her beautiful Olivia in the safe hands of the social services, she had asked him to look out for her but, in her what he'd thought must have been a bad state of mind, she hadn't said where she had left her.

Frank, on his return from the funeral, had found the letter and rang every social services office in the area and indeed the surrounding areas, looking for Olivia, not knowing she had been registered as Angel when there was no name on the letter attached to her cardigan.

Rose could see how hard Frank was finding this and she went to the cupboard and took out Billy's whiskey, it hadn't come out in a long time but she'd felt Frank needed a drink and he did.

He'd smiled and thanked her, "I have never given up on finding you. I always knew one day we would meet, somehow. I don't know it was just a feeling. I don't know how I never noticed the resemblance before.

"I mean, when we met at Jenny's house, you could be Moira sitting opposite me, she was beautiful." At that, he took out his wallet and showed them the last photo he'd had of his brother Tom and Moira, his wife on their wedding day, a note fell on the floor and Rose picked it up and handed it to him.

Angel looking at the photo, realised it was the first time she had seen her mother, gasped out loud. "I'm sorry, this must be so hard on you both." Frank opened the note that looked like it had been folded for years, the fold had shaped the paper and was sort of tearing as he opened it.

He smiled to himself. "Goodness, this is old. It's a letter I got from one of the social services offices all those years ago, funny it should turn up now, didn't even know it was there."

Angel hadn't been tuned in to what he had said, she was still looking at the old photograph from his wallet. It had been the first time she had laid eyes on her birth mother and she didn't feel anything; they were as strangers.

Chapter 6
A New Chapter in Her Life

Frank had handed the letter to Rose, who gasped as she read it, attracting Angel's attention. "Maggie," she'd said, looking at the signature at the end of the letter. Frank looked puzzled as he asked Rose if she'd known Maggie, he had never met the girl, he'd said, only on paper.

Rose explained how it was through a girl called Maggie that they had come to adopt Angel all those years ago. Probably a coincidence, she had concluded. The letter had said that Maggie had worked as a social worker in an office on the other side of town from where Moira and Tom had lived but had never had a child fitting the description of Olivia.

Frank, having contacted every social worker's office for miles around looking for Olivia as Moira had asked him to do, lived in hope. Maggie had done her research with his details but to no avail, he remembered opening the letter with shaking hands, hoping there might be hope, hoping at last he could find her and look after her for them.

Frank hadn't married himself, he was a career man, had thrown himself into his work with little time for anything else, a big mistake he had said, nothing to show for it, only a healthy bank account.

Money can't buy everything, he had said. Angel had felt a bit sorry for him, he seemed very much alone in the world, now they had found each other thankfully through Jenny's letter maybe that would change.

The evening had flown by with everyone's head bursting with information, Angel thought. Frank had spoken for hours about Angel's mum, of how they had been so excited when she was born.

He had been godfather to her and a friend of her mother's had been godmother, he wasn't sure where she was at the time and he couldn't even remember her name. They hadn't met before the christening day, so the name hadn't stuck in his mind but he'd kept all of Moira and Tom's stuff, so that Angel would probably find more information there if she wanted to have a look.

Due to return to work in a couple of days, Frank wanted to spend as much time with Angel as he could if that was ok with her. Angel was delighted to spend time with him, he was her link to her past.

Her past had never bothered her up to now but Jenny had changed all of that, she owed her a debt, there was no doubt about that. She would tend to their grave as a way to make it up to her.

She hoped Jenny's spirit was with her in her task of pursuing her past, she hoped she had granted her wish in finding Frank and taking it from there as she had put it in her letter.

Frank had sold Moira and Tom's house and furniture, however, there were personal things he didn't feel it right to get rid of. It was always his hope to find Olivia and pass their stuff on to her when she was old enough, stuff that was rightfully hers.

The sale of the house and furniture had brought a tidy sum, which too was put aside in the hope that he would find her. Angel was now a wealthy independent woman, unknowingly!

He would invite her to join him for maybe a little holiday and sort out some stuff, and of course, Rose was welcome as well. Angel was excited to arrange this as soon as she could; Rose, not one for flying, was a little more apprehensive but she would have to put her fears aside and do this for Angel.

It was a new chapter in her life after all and she was so happy to be a part of it, she could have decided to do it alone and that would have broken her heart. They had become more than mother and daughter, they were always the best of friends, and more so since Billy had passed.

Rose knew as she got up in the morning that this wasn't going to be a good day, she had the feeling of nerves in the pit of her stomach. A menopause thing! They would be flying at the weekend, what would she do if things kicked off that day, she hated this time of her life, her body wasn't her own, it had been taken over by this monster and she hardly recognised herself sometimes.

She would get so angry for no reason, she wanted to shout and shout and get this anger she was feeling, out for good. But that wasn't the way things would be, she would have to live with this for God knows how long, it was depressing.

As Angel packed her suitcase on her bed, she was shouting out to Rose who was doing the same in her bedroom, it was something they hadn't done in a long time. When she was a child, they had often gone on little trips but with work and everything, she just didn't seem to have the time of late, nor the interest.

It would be nice for her mother, she'd thought, to get away from it all for a few days. They would visit Billy before they left to say goodbye and tell him the story, there was so much to take in.

Sometimes, Angel would think it was all a dream, her finding her birth mother, and Jenny! The whole thing seemed unreal and they being buried in the same graveyard that she visited so often to talk to Billy. So much had come to light in the last few weeks and Jenny had brought this about.

As they got to the airport, Angel could see that Rose was nervous, she was putting a brave face on but Angel knew her too well, she knew she was a nervous traveller, so she did her best to reassure her that she would be safe.

A strong coffee to settle the nerves, she thought, so she left Rose to relax and she went to get the coffee. Rose was like a ghost, it was an awful thing to be nervous, Angel thought to herself, passing the coffee on to a very shaky hand.

Speaking about the flight, she assured her that more often than not the stuff we worry about never actually materialises, already the nervous type, she reckoned the menopause symptoms weren't helping things.

She hoped she would get on the plane when the time came, they had a couple of hours to wait to board which didn't help either! She had too much time for thinking. Finally seated in the plane, Angel could see Rose had such a tight grip on the armrest of the seat that her knuckles were white, the poor thing.

There wasn't a thing she could do to help other than to try to distract her. She had talked the whole way there though she'd thought a lot of the conversation had fallen on deaf ears, Rose was too stressed to take any of it in. She wasn't sure it was worth putting her through it but she didn't want to not include her either.

Maybe she could arrange a boat trip home instead, she would look into it, Frank might be able to help. Waiting at the arrivals as they walked out, Frank was so excited to see them, his house was about a twenty-minute drive away from the airport and he had organised for them to eat out in the evening after they had gotten a bit of a rest, he knew how travelling could be tiring.

Angel thought to herself, he was such a lovely man, how he never married she couldn't understand, surely he'd had many a chance, he was nice and easy on the eyes as well. After dinner, they chatted and Frank had asked her how the nursing was going, she explained how she hadn't returned to district nursing after Jenny and Brod had died, she'd found it too hard.

She was sort of in limbo at the moment, she had said and they left it at that. Rose got on well with Frank as well and he'd gone to so much effort to ensure their comfort while they visited, she'd said.

She was having a ball and was so happy to hear that Angel had arranged for them to return home by ferry. Frank would drive them to the port even though it was a couple of hours away but he didn't mind, he was only too happy to oblige.

Rose had spent the whole boat journey in the toilet, luckily, it wasn't the only toilet on the boat or there would have been many a one holding on to their water. Which was the worst of the two evils?

She didn't know, the flight or the boat trip! Home at last safe and sound, Rose looked worn out and dehydrated, she'd thrown up all the way home, a nice cup of tea, Angel thought, and bed for you.

She'd taken some of the stuff home from Frank's house that he'd held on to when he'd sold Moira and Tom's house, there was a lot of sorting to do and so much more that Frank was arranging to be sent to her. It was too much to take with her on her journey, he'd said.

He'd handed her a small box with some of her birth mother's belongings in it and said that in time, it would be precious to her. With the cases sorted and the washing in the machine, Angel decided to go through some of the stuff, a navy zipped bag with photographs and loose pages.

It felt a bit intrusive going through someone else's stuff, they were as strangers to her, it did indeed feel very strange. Sitting on the bed, she emptied the bag out and the first thing she picked up off the bed was a photo of a baby sitting on a lady's lap and looking up at her, obviously the baby was herself and the lady her mother.

Even though it was only an old photo, it was apparent that there was much love between the two. She felt a twinge of loneliness just then, she wasn't sure why but she'd felt at a loss.

She wondered what life would have been like being brought up by this beautiful lady, she could see the resemblance, there was no doubt. Quickly moving on as she could feel a lump in her throat, she picked up a loose page, it was a letter signed at the bottom, 'Love Mama' and there was a diary.

She wouldn't read it now, she thought, she would read it later, in among the other loose pages, she found an insurance policy never claimed, probably invalid by now, she'd thought. As she heard Rose moving around in the room next door, she called for her to come into her room and sit with her as she rummaged through the paperwork.

Rose suggested maybe reading the letter from her mother but Angel said she would leave it for another day, there was more than enough to deal with for now. There were a few more photographs, one of her christening day with Frank and her godmother, who she didn't know from Adam, and Moira and Tom.

Just like Frank in looks, very handsome, tall and with a kindly smile. Rose put her arm around her and hugged her, knowing how hard it must be but Angel told her it was ok and she was ok. There was a photograph of Jenny and Brod that took her back.

She'd never expected it. They were much younger in it but she'd know them anywhere, she'd said, showing it to Rose, the years had taken their toll on poor Jenny alright but then she had been heartbroken since the day Angel's mother took her own life, Brod had told her that. Things had never been the same since that awful day, he'd said he'd lost Jenny too, he'd lost her to grief.

It was a long time ago now and there was absolutely nothing anyone could do to bring them back, Angel knew she had been very lucky in life to have found Rose and Billy, and been loved as much if not more as if she had been reared by her birth mother and father.

It was getting all too much, she'd had enough for one day, she would put everything back into the bag and leave it for another day, it certainly was the beginning of a new chapter in her life; she would take one day at a time.

As she put the bag into her wardrobe, she could get a smell like perfume; she wasn't wearing perfume herself and Rose didn't wear perfume at all on any occasion as she was allergic, broke out in a rash if she wore it.

It couldn't be her mother's perfume after all those years, surely not, in talking to Rose downstairs, she suggested that maybe her mother had sprayed her perfume into the bag purposely to remind her of her smell.

Children recognise their mother's smell, she'd said and because the bag had been closed all these years, it may have lasted, who knows. She would never know now, there was so much of her past she didn't know but she was getting there, at least now she had Frank, a man she had never even known had existed until recently, thanks to Jenny.

She hoped Rose was really ok about all of this, nothing would ever change the way she felt about her adopted mother, nothing! Rose had said that she was happy for her to pursue things, it was after all her right, though she knew she had never shown an interest in finding her birth parents, it was the way it should be.

Jenny had put her on the path and she must follow wherever it would take her. She knew that nothing would ever change their relationship, no matter what she might find along the way, and it was exciting, she had told her.

Frank was working on getting the financial stuff organised, so he needed a few details on her adoption and her new name, etc. It would take a while to get it all sorted but it would leave her a woman of means.

He had been so very happy to do it and had waited such a long time, wondering if maybe he would never find her and both hers and his own wealth indeed would end up going to the state.

Now, he had someone to leave all of his worldly possessions to, he'd felt calm, his life now had more meaning, he wasn't alone in the world anymore. Frank had many friends, Jenny and Brod having been two of his most dearest in life, he had close colleagues and indeed lovely neighbours but now, he had family, he had Angel and Rose.

He would be forever indebted to Jenny for her suspicions and for sharing them with himself and Angel, a few simple words in a letter that would change his life forever.

Angel lay awake in bed, thinking about her life and how it had changed so much in a matter of weeks. Had she not taken up district nursing and gone to travel with her career behind her like Shelly and lots of her other friends, then she wouldn't have ever met Jenny and Brod.

Was life's journey laid out for one, she'd thought, maybe the gods had led her to her nursing career so that she would meet Jenny and Brod, how else was she going to find her roots! It was all too much of a coincidence, there had to be something.

Worn out from thinking, she'd finally fallen asleep to be awoken next morning by the sound of the phone ringing in the hallway, Rose had shouted up the stairs to say that Frank was on the phone.

As she got out of bed, she tripped over the belt of her dressing gown that was trailing on the floor; half asleep, she picked herself up and ran down the stairs, hoping she hadn't kept Frank too long waiting.

She needn't have worried. Rose had been keeping him in conversation and was laughing as she handed the phone to her. "He's so nice," she said as she turned and walked away, leaving Angel to chat in private.

Apologising for keeping him on hold, Angel listened attentively to Frank's news, he had been to his solicitor and signed everything over to Angel, he'd hesitated for a moment and went on to say that he'd also made his will.

He had named her as the sole beneficiary of his worldly belongings and he was so delighted with himself, her money would be transferred into her account within the week. She was shaking as she hung up the phone; it was a lot of money, somehow it didn't seem right but it was apparently rightfully hers.

It would take a while to sink in, as she discussed it with Rose, she could see the happiness light up her face, she was indeed so happy for her, and so happy that things had turned out ok for her.

She would be set up for life now, independent and able to do whatever she pleased, her dear dad Billy would be so happy too, she'd told her. Rose had said that from wherever he was watching and she was sure that he was, he would be so proud of their daughter.

Angel would always have done well in life, Rose thought, she was a hard worker and such a dependable person that any employer would be proud to have her work for them. But now, she would have a choice as to what she wanted to do with her life, she had been set up well and whether it was fate or just luck that sent it her way, she was so happy for her.

Angel was walking around in a daze for a while, this was a strange sort of feeling, having money in the bank! Normally, she was waiting for her wages to go in at the beginning of the month, by the last week of the month, she would be counting the pennies usually. It sure was a different sort of a feeling. She would go to the graveyard and talk to Billy, let him know her news, she would feel better then.

A cold and damp day the graveyard seemed drearier than ever, she'd told Billy about her situation and asked him to guide her. She felt a warm feeling come over her as if he had hugged her, she missed him so much, as she turned to go, she decided to visit Jenny and Brod's grave.

Maybe have a little chat with Jenny and tell her how she had pursued her suspicions as she had wished her to do and of course, the outcome. Walking to Jenny and Brod's grave, she would have to pass by Moira and Tom's resting place.

She'd stood there with Frank already but it had been a blur, she had been so out of it with the stress of it all at that time. Now, as she walked towards the grave, she felt she needed to thank them for setting her up for life, and maybe ask them why! Tom, having died at a very young age of natural causes, had had no choice in leaving her but her mother, why?

Thought to be in a state of depression according to Frank, she wasn't held responsible for her actions at the time, this was so hard to imagine for Angel, how could a person leave a small child to the mercy of others.

Would she ever understand, she had studied depression in her college days and she should understand but reading about it and experiencing it in real life were two completely different things. How it must take such a hold on you that you would take your own life was so very sad.

Standing by their graves, her feelings were as ever, as in she'd felt nothing, no sadness, no connection with them; nevertheless, she would look after their resting place, bring flowers and keep it tidy.

They were after setting her up for life, it was the least she could do; walking away, she did feel a tinge of sadness, she wasn't sure why, maybe it was because they were such sad circumstance surrounding their deaths according to what Frank had told her.

Whether one knew them or not, their story would bring a lump in one's throat, not to mind being related. She walked to Jenny and Brod's grave and talked to them for a while, she wished Jenny had told her sooner about her suspicions about her being Moira's daughter, maybe they could have talked about it, maybe even things might have ended differently!

As she drove up the road and parked outside, Angel noticed the front door was open, no sign of Rose in the garden; it was very unusual for her to be in the house with the door open. She could hear chatter as she walked up the path.

"Angel, come in, come in. Frank has just arrived out of the blue." Rose was all excited to see him. Angel left her bag in the hallway and hurried into the kitchen, she too was excited to see Frank.

He hadn't mentioned coming home when she had spoken to him on the phone only a few days previous. She knew by the look on his face that he had something to tell her, she just knew it. Rose busied herself with the kettle, leaving them to chat.

Frank stood with his arms out, inviting her for a hug, it was the first time he'd done that and Angel had felt a bit awkward. Pointing to the kitchen table, she offered him a chair, there was something on his mind alright.

As he sat at the table, he took a letter out of his jacket pocket but before he declared what was in the letter, he'd said he'd wanted to talk to her in person, this wasn't something they could discuss over the phone.

Angel was totally confused at this stage, apologising to begin with, he'd gone on to say that seemingly when they had come for a visit, herself and Rose, Angel had left her hairbrush behind or rather, he'd said he'd taken it out of the bathroom and held onto it.

Wondering why, Angel had thought perhaps he'd wanted something of hers to remember her by but surely not. Definitely not as it turned out!

Frank and Angel's birth mother, Moira had gotten close over the years, very close. Tom, unaware of any carrying on, was busy with his work, away a lot of the time, leaving Moira on her own at home.

Frank would visit regularly and Moira always insisted on him staying with them, there was a spare room and why would he be forking out money to hotels when there was no need and besides, it was his home after all.

All ears, Rose stood in shock at the sink, it was obvious what he was going to say next, he'd kept the hairbrush to have it checked for DNA.

"I'd always had my suspicions, Angel. I searched and searched for you all those years. I had to know for sure. Moira had never questioned you being Tom's daughter but I don't know. I always wondered and when I found you, it was the happiest day of my life.

"I had to know and so too do you have a right to know, the results are there. I should have asked for your permission, I know," handing Angel the already opened letter, Frank got up and walked around the room, looking so troubled.

He'd gone on to say that if the result was otherwise and Tom had been her birth father, he wasn't going to mention the test at all, but he thought she had the right to know. He was her biological father!

First, her parents' estate that left her a woman of means and now, her father wasn't her father at all! Angel couldn't digest it all, she went back out into the car and started to drive, taking the letter with her.

Rose was sitting in silence, when she got back, the radio was off and there wasn't a sign of Frank. He'd checked into a B&B nearby and would call Angel in the morning, said maybe they could talk, he hadn't said much to Rose after Angel took off, only to apologise for upsetting them.

Angel hugged her mother and cried and cried, she'd let it all out, the build-up of the last few months all going round in her head, she was near breaking point; she wanted to be back where Rose and Billy were the only parents she knew and life was simple, it was getting all too complicated now.

Waking with a throbbing headache not having had much sleep, Angel got out of bed staggering, she would shower and have a cup of tea and face the day. Frank was due to call, whether that would be in person or on the phone, she wasn't too sure, he hadn't said, she would have to wait and see.

There was so much to think about and her head was already bursting with a headache. Rose could see that she was struggling and suggested maybe going for a walk, it was a lovely fresh day and the air would clear her head, she would stay in case Frank called.

Walking through the meadow, Angel felt revived, her hair blowing in the cool breeze had refreshed her in no time and she found she could think clearly again.

Rose and Billy were the only parents she had known, they would always be her mum and dad as far as she was concerned and only for what Jenny had said in her note, Angel would have been none the wiser.

There were three words going around in her head. 'Ignorance is bliss'. There were no truer words. Knowing what she knew now however, she would have to face the truth, it was written in black and white. Frank was her biological father.

Was it a once off or had her mother been having an affair with her uncle as she thought Frank was. This was going to be a tough conversation but one that had to be aired, walking towards the house, Angel had made her mind up.

She would go on as she always did, being as she always was, a caring person happy within herself and content within her life, all of this upset from Jenny and Brod taking their own lives to Jenny's note to her on her death, to meeting Frank and finding out he was her biological father, all of this was eating her up inside.

It had to stop, it was what it was and she would have to accept it and get on with it, she'd lost her job that she had loved because of it and had become a person she hardly recognised anymore.

Apologising to Frank for walking out the evening before, she hugged him and offered him tea. He'd been chatting to Rose when she came back from her walk and both looked very concerned when she walked in and so relieved at the same time.

They'd talked for hours, Rose wanting to leave the room to let them talk but Angel asking her to stay; she wanted her mother there, she wanted her to be a part of whatever was to come.

As it turned out, it hadn't been a one-off get-together between Moira and Frank. He'd remembered thinking when he heard that Tom and Moira found they were going to have a baby that he hadn't seen both of them since that night when he and Moira had decided to call it a day, the deceit was killing him and he couldn't go on.

He really had feelings for Moira, ashamed to admit that what he'd felt for her was very strong and it wasn't right. The thought had crossed his mind straight away, it could have been his baby. Tom had been away with work and Frank had stayed over in their house.

They'd had a few too many drinks and well, as he said, the rest was history. Moira had never suspected that the baby wasn't Tom's, and neither did Tom. But all the while, Frank had said that something told him the baby was his. It had always niggled at him, his instincts were spot on!

Frank would be retiring in a couple of years and had said he had always planned on moving back home when he retired, he wondered if Angel would be ok with having him living close by.

There was nothing concrete yet, not even a date of his retirement but if he had thought that Angel would be at all uncomfortable with him living nearby, then that wouldn't happen. He'd upset the apple cart enough to do a lifetime already.

Angel assured him that there would no problem at all, she wouldn't dream of upsetting his plans to retire in an area where he'd grown up, what right she had to do that in the first place.

It wasn't Frank's plan to upset things, she liked Frank; he was a kind good hearted person and what life had brought about wasn't entirely of his doing, Moira should surely have had some suspicions back then.

No, she had to accept things as they were, life was too short, Billy used to say that to her when she'd fall out with one of her friends at school and it was true. Sometimes, we have to just get on with it.

She would go to visit Billy and take Rose shopping for a treat, this must have taken its toll on her as well although she hadn't said anything. Frank would be heading home on the six o clock train, she would drop him at the station and go straight to the graveyard.

Having talked to Billy, she'd felt a weight lift from her mind, while Rose was busying herself with tidying the pots that had blown all over the place, Angel looked on and thanked her lucky stars for having been raised by such lovely people.

Where Frank would fit into the equation, she wasn't sure at that stage, she would let nature take its course; for now, she had to get back to making a life for herself and Rose, she would think about going back to nursing, or maybe not!

It sure had turned out a new chapter in her life, who'd have known six months previous when collecting her dressings and looking after her patients was her main priority that things would change so drastically. It was like another life, could she go back to that?

She wasn't sure but one thing she did know was that she had to be doing something. Ok, she could afford now not to work for the rest of her life, just live off her inheritance but when she thought back to her hard studying to get her degree and the pride in both Billy and Roses' eyes on the day she graduated, she couldn't waste that.

She had loved nursing, perhaps in a different area of nursing, maybe paediatric, who knows. There was a place for her out there, she just had to find it and she was determined that she would. The past belonged in the past, she must now look to the future.

Taking the withered flowers from Rose, she turned to go, helping Rose through the bumpy grass that surrounded the grave, all of a sudden, she wanted to go to Moira and Tom's grave.

Only a stone's throw from Billy's grave, Rose was glad to see her take an interest, the last few months and the rollercoaster of emotions that followed must have been so hard on her, she thought.

Though smiling on the outside, God only knows what turmoil she was dealing with on the inside. Of course, they went to visit Jenny and Brod's grave as well.

Rose felt as if she'd known them all her life, Angel had told her so much about them since that awful tragic day, a day that had changed all of their lives forever.

Chapter 7
Do What You Want When You Want

Angel knew she had decisions to make and she would struggle to make them probably, but nothing had to be decided right away, Rose had said as they sat watching the burning flames of the open fire.

It had been a bitterly cold day and Rose had spent the afternoon baking, the kitchen had a homely smell of apple tart in the oven and scones already baked, cooling on the table. The fire was lit early and the room was cosy.

Rose thought to herself that there was only one thing missing to make it perfect, if only Billy was there. They both missed him terribly, though spoken about every day and happy memories shared, there was a void in their lives that no one else could ever fill.

It worried Rose a bit that Angel was spending so much time alone, no interest in meeting up with her friends though with them all working away, it was impossible anyway but she did worry a bit. What if something were to happen to her?

Frank had settled back to work though his heart wasn't in it, since he'd uncovered the truth about Angel or Olivia as he had known her in the past, he was constantly thinking about her.

Of the wasted years he had lost with her and the longing he'd had for so long to be a part of her life, he'd always known that the baby was his, there was just something in his heart telling him that for years.

He didn't want to waste any more time, his work that he had lived for all those years now seemed irrelevant, fate had brought him here, he'd found his daughter and nothing else mattered.

Though planning his retirement within a couple of years anyway, he had thoughts of bringing it forward a bit, a good bit as in right away!

Maybe find a place where he could see Angel every day, though knowing lost time is never found again, he'd hoped that the future might give him the chance to make it up to her, even a bit of it.

How anyone could take her own life and leave her baby to the mercy of strangers, to him seemed inconceivable, he'd lived his life with the weight of this on his shoulders, his strength almost spent.

It wasn't a story he could share with a workmate, the only people he could share his grief with were now gone, dear Jenny and Brod. They'd helped him through some of the worst moments of his life.

A life lived accompanied only by sadness, until now. He wasn't going to waste another minute! Angel too had thoughts of Frank, she'd only known him as a friend of Jenny and Brod's until recently, when a simple letter from a dear lady, a patient of hers on her daily route who she had so enjoyed visiting, had changed her life forever and whether she liked it or not, this was so and only time would tell the outcome.

She remembered when herself and Katie, her best friend all through school, would talk about growing up and working hard and maybe meet someone rich, so that they could travel the world and live in luxury all of their lives.

They would laugh and imagine being able to afford fancy clothes, maybe a fancy car. Those were the days, she'd thought, not a care in the world, as if silly things like fancy clothes and fancy cars were important.

She now knew that it's only when you grow up and realise that your loved ones won't always be there, that's when you know what's important in life and fancy clothes or fancy cars don't even come close.

She had a thought, she had wondered what she would do with her inheritance, sure she would look after Rose and they could live quite comfortably for the rest of their days on it but she wanted to do more.

It had been going round in her head for a while now, as much as she loved her nursing, she just couldn't see herself going back there, it would be too hard.

She had in the past considered going on to do a master's but there was no way she could have afforded it and though Billy and Rose would have raised the money in some way if they had known her thoughts, she'd thought they'd put enough into her career at that stage, it was time she'd started to earn and pay them back some of what they had spent on her education. Now, she could afford it!

Rose thought it was a great idea, she needed something, she was spending too much time thinking and trying to make sense of it all, this was perfect. She would return as a mature student, which in itself would be a challenge but she did love a challenge.

It was like the stars were aligned, as if someone was looking out for her! She got her place in college within an hour's drive of where they lived and couldn't wait to get started.

Parking in the students' car park just a short walk away from the entrance, Angel felt queasy all of a sudden and her legs wouldn't move, they felt like jelly, she felt sick. Looking around at the students as they walked together in groups, laughing and confident looking, she wondered what she was thinking!

She was so much older than most of them, at least ten if not fifteen years, but then as if like magic, a calmness came over her, she found herself walking towards the entrance and going up the steps to accept this challenge.

Where she had gotten the strength from she wasn't sure but on her way home, she stopped in at Billy's grave to chat to him and thank him, she was sure it was he who took her hand that morning, she just felt it.

It all felt very strange, back to timetables and study but she was proud of herself for the first time in ages; she would give this her all and when she took out her masters, it would open up so many more doors to her.

Rose had an apple tart on the table cooling, she hadn't heard Angel come in and she was singing in the kitchen. Angel hadn't heard her sing in so long. Billy used to say she hadn't a note in her head and wink at Angel and go to Rose and pick her up and swing her round while she proceeded to hit him with her tea towel.

They were such a loving couple and she had such lovely childhood memories, she would be forever grateful to them, she missed Billy so much.

There was a letter addressed to Angel left on the table beside the apple tart, she recognised the handwriting, it was Frank's. She never referred to him as her father or even her uncle, just Frank, perhaps in time!

He had taken retirement and was looking at moving home as he called it, though years living away, this was always home to him. She'd read the letter aloud to Rose who thought it was grand that he was moving home and retiring; after all, he was getting on and there was no point in waiting until age caught up and you were left no choice but to retire.

Angel smiled at her and she went on to say it was true. "Retire while you can enjoy life and the freedom of doing what you want when you want." Angel agreed, life was too short!

The course was proving difficult, intense with a combination of modules, seminars and lectures, not to mention individual research. Angel was finding it exhausting but in a very gratifying way, she had gotten to know new people though most half her age, they had accepted and included her.

Public health nursing now seemed a lifetime ago, that part of her life was now in the past and she had to bury all of the sadness that went with it; though she would never forget Jenny and Brod, she would have to try to remember the good times she had with them, the chats and laughs and bury the awful memory that still pierced her heart.

She would never make sense of it if she was to dwell on it forever, she had done that for a long time to the extent that it was making her ill. How they must have planned it all so well, down to the weather on that night.

It had to be bitter cold for their plan to work, cold enough to die of hyperthermia overnight. It made her shiver to this day!

Rose, still struggling with 'the change' as she called it, herself seemed to have a new lease on life since Angel went back to college, walking to the cemetery on a fine day, stopping off in the shops on the way home for a few bits.

Chatting to neighbours, no doubt Angel being the topic of conversation, as she overheard her one day when she passed her by at the gate while she chatted to a neighbour. She was so proud and Angel was so happy to give her something to be proud about.

It seemed like with Angel now settled and getting on with her life that she too could get on with hers, she'd said that once she'd accepted her symptoms of menopause, they didn't seem as bad, it was like her body was fighting it and making it worse.

She had laughed and said that getting old wasn't all that bad after all. As she listened to the voice on the other end of the phone, a shiver ran down her back, Frank had put in an offer for a house nearby and it had been accepted, they would soon be neighbours.

He could hardly contain his excitement while Angel on the other hand had felt anxious, sure she was delighted that Frank got to move back home to enjoy his retirement, she was happy for him and told him as much, though maybe not with as much enthusiasm as he!

Would this change everything again? She had accepted that he was her biological father but at a distance, it was like he was miles away and she didn't have to deal with it. Having him close by meant maybe seeing him every day, having to deal with her past.

That which she had not as yet dealt with, it was so much easier to leave it in the past. Rose questioned her fears when she told her that Frank would soon be their neighbour, her thoughts on the situation were so different. Frank was such a nice man and so eager to get to know his daughter.

She'd had no idea that Angel had felt such anxiety, while she understood that it was the saddest story she had ever heard that a mother so distressed with life that she would take her own life rather than face it and leave her beautiful daughter behind, but as she did when she'd first heard about it, she assured Angel that her mother wasn't in a good place to do a thing like that and she wasn't to blame.

There had been very little said about it after that and when it did come up in conversation, it was only in passing. Angel never wanted to talk about her past, now she knew why, it actually scared her.

Surely, Rose had thought that carrying this around in her head wasn't doing her any good, it was a weight in itself. She remembered the social worker Maggie had said that Angel had always seemed uptight as if waiting and missing someone, it had taken a long time for her to settle and sometimes, she wouldn't settle at all.

Rose remembered her playing on the floor when they'd fostered her first and every time the door would open, she would stop what she was doing and with the biggest, saddest eyes, she would look to see who was coming in.

Often turning round as if disappointed with a tear in her eye. Knowing what she knew now it wasn't any wonder, she must have missed her mother and her father. She must have wondered where they had gone and why all of a sudden that she was among strangers.

Rose had always felt for her though she didn't know the full story, she knew that her little girl was lonely, she had been much loved and she was missing someone. The sadness in her eyes had stayed for a long time but when the day came that at last she seemed to accept them, she would run to them with so much love that it had often brought a tear to her eye, a tear of happiness.

She remembered Billy would call her soft, in the nicest of ways. She had often caught Billy wipe a tear from his eye quietly too but she would never remark. Children have a way of pulling at the heart strings that no other can do, it's like they're attached in some way and when things go wrong or even when things go right, it affects you too.

She missed Billy, he would know what to say, he would have sorted Angel's fears by now, he wouldn't have let her past cause her anxiety, he would have talked about it. Angel was happy to leave her past in the past and though Rose knew that at some stage, she would have to deal with it, she was happy to do that also because she didn't know what to advise her, Billy would have known.

There had been many new opportunities open to her in taking on her masters and she had considered most of them, the one that appealed to her most was the nurse midwife. It meant a longer course and a lot of study but it would be worth it.

In speaking with her career advisory officer, it was decided and it was the best decision she had ever made, she loved it. A career so rewarding, so privileged, preparing a woman for the birth of her child, a new life.

With every birth, she had felt every bit as excited as the parents of the new-born. Of course, there were difficult days as well, there were days when difficult choices had to be made, mothers choosing not to have treatment for a disease that could kill them, for the sake of the unborn baby.

Babies born stillborn, many heart wrenching days watching parents who had longed to hold their baby in their arms, only to have their precious child stillborn. There were days she would ask why?

But then there were days that she would wonder at the miracle of seeing a baby being born, it was magical. Yes, she had chosen well and the study, the lectures, the working into the early hours, all worth it in the end.

Then there was the expense, the fees that she would never have been able to afford if it wasn't for her inheritance. Whatever she'd thought of her mother abandoning her as a child, and in her mind, now she felt that she had dealt with it, she wouldn't be in her position or have her career only for her inheritance.

Her mother most likely suffered with depression and finding her husband dead beside her in bed that day most likely drove her to the edge. It's funny, she'd thought to herself but one never knows what's going on in someone's head, they may seem bright and cheerful on the outside but struggling on the inside.

Rose had organised a counselling session for her after hearing that Frank was moving home and seeing how anxious Angel seemed, she'd even attended it with her on the first session.

It had taken quite a few sessions before she was able to talk openly about her feelings, going right back to her feeling of loss, which she could never explain. It just all came pouring out and had left her exhausted.

Sybil and Lawrence were such a lovely couple, four weeks before her due date, Sybil developed high blood pressure and the birth was brought forward because of concerns for both the mother and baby. All went well and they had a beautiful baby boy.

Angel thought that the name they chose was so unusual. They named him Ralph, not named for any of their relations just a name that they chose because they liked the sound of it and they had given it lots of thought.

Watching them walk proudly down the corridor with Lawrence carrying their little boy in his car seat and Sybil linking him and looking into the baby as she walked, Angel felt proud too, proud to have been a part of the birth nursing and caring for Sybil and her new baby and supporting the new dad as he cried openly with joy.

They were so nice, Sybil turning back to wave as Lawrence held the door for her as they went. Rose could see the joy in Angel's face as she got up every morning to go to work, she was so happy for her. At last, she had found her calling in life and she deserved every bit of happiness she had found.

Frank, now well settled in his new home, would call by every now and then and the tension had passed. Angel had accepted him as her birth father though she would often say that Billy was her real dad and always would be her number one.

As they sat round the table, Rose would often watch as she stirred the gravy or got up to get more roast potatoes, and she could plainly see the resemblance between Frank and Angel. It was undeniable not so much in their looks, although at times she could see a little resemblance there as well but in their ways.

She would often invite him round for dinner on a Sunday, she liked to make a special effort on a Sunday. Do a nice roast with all the trimmings and gravy, of course. Angel loved her gravy even as a child, there would be gravy with every dinner.

Sunday was a nice easy day, no one had to be up for work and the chores were done for the week, Billy always believed in putting down tools as he used to say and taking a breather on a Sunday. Monday would come round soon enough and we would be back to the grinding stone he used to say. She missed Billy so.

It was a beautiful day and Angel decided to take her lunch to the park nearby and take in a few rays. Rose had packed a lunch for two or more as usual, as often as she would say that one sandwich was plenty, she would still do at least three.

"Sure, you might be hungry," she would say with a smile. Angel would always kiss her goodbye and tell her that she loved her. She appreciated how lucky she was to have her lunch prepared for her every day, her dinner on the table when she got home and her laundry taken care of.

There had been many discussions about her laundry and how she would prefer that her mother would sit down and put her feet up and she herself would look after the laundry but it always fell on deaf ears.

She breathed a sigh of relief to sit on the bench in the park, it was so nice to kick her shoes off and relax for a while, it had been a very busy morning. As he walked past with the baby in the buggy, she recognised Lawrence. He seemed miles away as she said hello.

Turning back to join her on the bench, he seemed so happy to see her, baby Ralph was sleeping, now about six months old, she reckoned. A beautiful baby, so peaceful in sleeping, so handsome, could be looking at a miniature of his dad, a very handsome man as well.

Nothing could have prepared her for what he had to tell her, it had left her speechless and hardly able to get on with her work for the rest of the day. With tears in his eyes, he had explained how they had lost Sybil, settling in to family life with their beautiful baby, there had been much to do as the baby had come earlier than planned.

They worked so hard to get his crib and baby bits that they needed and enjoyed every minute of it, it had been a struggle with climbing three flights of stairs up in their apartment and the rent had taken most of their spare cash at the end of the month but they both agreed that money wasn't everything.

In the grand scheme of things, they were millionaires. Ralph was their everything and they couldn't be happier. When Ralph was about six weeks old, Lawrence having returned to work, Sybil would spend most of the day looking at him while he slept.

Lawrence had said that he would often return from work to find the breakfast things still on the table and they would laugh about it. When he would get home, they would both spend most of the evening looking at the miracle that was Ralph.

It was a Friday evening and he had rang Sybil before he left work to see if she needed anything picking up in the shops but she hadn't answered the phone. Not thinking anything of it, he continued on home, parking in the basement of the apartment block as usual.

As he approached their landing three flights up, he promised himself he would get back into training, he could hardly catch his breath. He could hear the baby crying as he put the key in the door, Sybil was lying on the floor and the baby was lying between her legs as if she had been holding him when she fell ill.

It was confirmed that she had had a seizure, her blood pressure was high and she would have to be taken into the hospital for tests. They had mentioned what they had thought might be the cause of the seizure but Lawrence wasn't taking it in.

He would have to ring home and get his mother to come and mind Ralph while he followed the ambulance. Only living a few minutes away, his mother was there in a flash, taking Ralph into her arms, she told Lawrence not to delay but to get to Sybil's bedside as soon as he could.

She would be frightened, she had said but he knew by the look in her eyes that there was something she wasn't telling him. His mother was a retired nurse who had worked her way up to staff nurse, and had a very successful career while his grandmother had more or less reared him.

He knew that she was concerned about Sybil with the fact that she had just had a baby and though rare, they all knew the dangers that a pregnancy could bring, before and after the birth.

To Lawrence, Sybil seemed just fine, she was enjoying looking after Ralph, she hadn't been overdoing it or anything because he wouldn't have let her, although only five weeks old and never having looked after a baby before, they'd thought that they were doing well and managing the baby well.

He was confused and in shock and probably not in a state to be driving but he'd had no other choice, he had to get there and fast.

Chapter 8
Life Could Be So Cruel

There was panic in the room as he approached, Lawrence had said, not going into much detail, he continued that Sybil had never regained consciousness that day. She'd developed sepsis and had renal failure and there was no hope, though they had done everything they could, it was too late.

He'd tormented himself for a long time, believing that had he not gone to work that day, things might have been different, he might not have lost her.

It was killing him that he hadn't noticed that anything was wrong in the morning he'd left her in bed with Ralph in her arms, the consultant had said she'd had a seizure most likely from high blood pressure.

But she hadn't complained, only to say that she'd had a headache the evening before, which wasn't out of the ordinary for Sybil as she had suffered from migraines most of her life. She wasn't in the least bit worried about it and nor was he.

She was an awful loss to them and though only a few months down the road, he wasn't sure he could deal with it all. Everyone was so kind and all reassured him that time would heal but he wasn't feeling any healing, if anything he'd felt worse as time went on.

Ralph was beginning to take notice and for some reason, he would wake every night at the same time, two o clock in the morning. It was the loneliest time, he would cry along with him until they would both fall asleep in Sybil's rocking chair.

She'd spotted it in the window of a mother and baby shop in the high street and though money was tight, he'd got it for her for her birthday, with only a couple of months to go before the baby was due, it had made her so happy.

Hardly able to speak, Angel wished him well and told him she would be there for him should he ever want a friend, it was a dreadful state of affairs altogether. Goodness, life could be so cruel, she'd thought.

She'd hoped no one would notice her tears as she headed back to work, her heart was breaking for him. It had been the longest afternoon, she couldn't get Lawrence and the baby out of her head.

That poor beautiful little boy would never get to know his mother, never get to cuddle with her or get to know her smell. It had brought to mind the smell she had got from the little cardigan Rose had given her, was it her own mother's smell?

She had been wearing it when she was left outside the social worker's office, Rose had kept it for so long for her in the hope that one day, it would mean something to her. There was definitely a smell of perfume on it, it hadn't stirred anything in her as such but she did often wonder.

She was probably too young to remember her mother's smell, though it did comfort her at times just to hold it, hug it even. She'd thought about her mother for a few moments, her birth mother.

She wasn't sure why, perhaps it was the situation with Lawrence and the baby, now left without a mother and she remembered what Frank had said about Moira not being able to cope. She hoped Lawrence wouldn't go down that road, though she was sure he wouldn't but then they say it's a thin line, she thought to herself.

Frank had pulled up outside as Rose was taking the rubbish to the bin, she watched as he came up the pathway, noticing he was dragging his leg. He'd twisted his knee getting out of the car the day before and he'd said he hadn't slept a wink the night before with the pain of it.

Angel had just come out of the shower and was wrapping her wet hair in a towel when Rose shouted up the stairs to tell her that the dinner was ready and that Frank had arrived. She'd thought he looked tired and pale but didn't like to pass remarks until Rose told her about Frank twisting his leg.

She remembered she'd had a knee support from a while back and offered it to him for support in case he'd injured it, which he obviously had. Wrapping it round his knee, she noticed he had a birth mark on the calf of his leg, in the exact same spot as she had herself.

In being with him of late and getting to know him better over the time, she'd had no doubt they'd had a lot in common and now the same birth mark, Frank was definitely her birth father.

Though she had accepted it long since in her head, she thought to herself that maybe it was time to show it outwardly. He had never put pressure on her in any way for confirmation of her accepting him, and neither did she ever acknowledge the fact. Maybe it was time!

As she got into the car next morning with the windscreen all fogged up and the smell of damp in the car, she swore she would get rid of the car next day she was off.

There was obviously water coming in somewhere, the back seat felt damp and cold and more often than not the boot would have water in it. She missed Billy for stuff like that, he would have had it sorted right away.

Her mind was made up, she would take Rose with her to look at some new cars and maybe ask Frank to come along too. He would know an awful lot more about cars than they would.

She wasn't fussy, just something with wheels that didn't leak in the rain that would do, she wasn't into the glamour of the fancy cars, just something dependable that didn't cost too much. Though she was left comfortable, she would never be extravagant, Billy had taught her to think of the rainy day.

Frank was only too delighted to go along, still hobbling with his sore knee, they'd drove for hours and looked at so many cars that she was more confused than anything at the end of the day. Frank would scrutinise and after the salesman going into every detail, he would walk away.

Angel was beginning to get embarrassed but trusted that he knew what he was doing. Eventually, there was a car that seemed to please, all that was left to do was to get Angel's approval.

She loved it, sitting in the front seat and looking around it with the lovely new smell of leather, she was so proud, she thought of Billy and wondered if he would approve. He too would have been fussy, wouldn't be one to part with money lightly, he would get the best value available.

Then she thought of Moira and Tom, both of whom had made this possible for her, they'd secured her future for her and she was grateful. There would be no need for finance companies getting involved or paying back loans, she would be paying in cash and did indeed feel privileged in being able to do so.

She wasn't sure if it was that she was getting older or what but she'd felt no bitterness against her birth mother now, all of that had passed. She no longer held on to those thoughts, she had been luckier than most in having been adopted by Rose and Billy and having had a happy childhood.

Holding on to stuff that in the end only weighs you down was silly and it was past time to move on. She would visit Moira and Tom's grave and of course, Billy's and Jenny and Brod's. She could spend the day in that place and often did, always coming away feeling empty and sad.

It was a pleasure to drive her new car, Rose sat, looking really proud in the passenger seat. They took it for a long drive at the weekend and had a bit of lunch in a pub on the way. They hadn't done that for a while and it was lovely.

Between work and getting home late some evenings, they hadn't had much time to talk recently, Angel found herself discussing Frank and Moira and Tom, the whole messy situation with Rose.

It felt like a weight had lifted when they got up to go, she hugged her mother and thanked her for listening. Rose was beginning to show her age, Angel thought, she was getting on a bit but seemed to be coping a bit better with her menopause symptoms these days.

She wondered what she would do if anything were to happen to her, she would be lost without her, totally lost. Theirs was a bond so strong, were she her birth mother, Angel didn't think she could love her any more.

She wouldn't think about that now, it had been a lovely day and her mother was there beside her, she would appreciate every minute she had with her as she always did. Frank was on their heels when they got home, anxious to hear how she'd managed the new car, she thanked him for his help once more and offered to take him round the block for a spin to get the feel of it.

He was in the passenger seat before she'd finished the sentence. As they drove past the cemetery, she asked if he would mind waiting for her if she went in to say hello.

Frank wondered if maybe he could accompany her, standing at her mother and Tom's grave, she wondered if Frank felt it strange, he had to; after all, Tom was his brother, he'd taken advantage of Moira being on her own while Tom worked away all those years ago.

Never having got the chance to face him about it or clear the air as it were, not having found out for sure that he was her dad until Moira's letter. Angel could see that he was deep in thought as she looked over at him.

Noticing her looking at him, he winked at her and started to walk away, walking out of the graveyard, he hadn't said a word but as he held the gate open for Angel as she walked out, he looked back and with a tear in his eye, he said, "I hope peace finds her."

Angel thought this a strange thing to say but then she hadn't known her birth mother, obviously there was more to her story than she knew but that was for another day. Very impressed with the new car, Frank wished her luck and safe driving.

He decided to keep going as they got out of the car, although she had expected he would go in for a cup of tea, but he seemed a bit thoughtful, so she thanked him for his wishes and said goodbye.

Rose was disappointed that he hadn't come in, she had made an apple tart and had whipped some fresh cream. It was so nice to come home to that wonderful smell of home cooking.

Rose was listening closely as Angel told her of the visit to the graveyard, she too thought it an unusual thing to say but also agreed that they didn't know the true story, perhaps Moira had other problems. Maybe someday, Frank would discuss it with her.

Work was as busy as ever and though she loved every minute of it, Angel was finding it exhausting, she would be in bed early. Funny, she thought to herself, she could chat until all hours with Rose and not feel tired at all, yet by early afternoon at work, she was dragging her feet.

Late nights and early mornings don't go, Rose had told her, it was alright for her, she could take the weight off and have a cup of tea anytime of the day at home but when you clock into a job, you are expected to keep going, especially in the job and career Angel had chosen.

It was a tough one but very rewarding, she could see she was happy in it and seemed very content with her life, she still wished that she would socialise more, her young life was passing her by.

The weekend had only arrived and it was gone. Angel couldn't believe it was Monday again, seemed only like a minute ago that it was Friday evening and she was looking forward to the break, a well-earned break.

The sister on the maternity ward was waiting for her when she arrived at work, she was early, so it wasn't a telling off she'd hoped. As it happened, the lady that she had looked after the previous week had left her a letter on her discharge the day before and sister was to hand it to her personally.

As she put her coat into her locker and prepared for her day, Angel put the letter into her bag and said she would read it at home later.

After a full run down of her day at work with Rose who took such an interest in Angel's day, it was time for a shower and a bit of relaxing, it was a lovely bright evening and she thought to herself she might go for a little stroll after the dinner, she loved the long evenings.

As she took her bag from the post at the foot of the stairs where she always threw it as she came in after work, the car keys thrown in the ashtray on the hall table, it was all automatic, she didn't even think.

Often the front door would be left open if the evening was nice or maybe the smoke alarm went off as it always did when they'd use the grill, the letter fell onto the floor. Her bag was open, she really did need to be more careful with her stuff.

What was to stop anyone pinching her bag in passing when the door was open, they wouldn't even notice from the kitchen. She opened the letter as she walked up the stairs to change and have a shower.

Penny was a single mother, somehow they had clicked right away and become friends in the short time they'd known each other. Her beautiful baby girl was born prematurely and had been kept for a while longer after Penny's discharge.

She was so thankful for the help and care that Angel had given her at such a traumatic time in her life and she would never forget her, she hoped she would bump into her again while visiting her baby in the coming days but just in case she wouldn't see her again, she wanted to thank her personally.

Though she had already decided on a name for her little girl, she would give her the name Angel as her second name.

That way, she had said, she would always remember her. Angel was so touched by her words, after all, she was there to help and care, that was her job but it was nice to hear that she was doing it well.

Frank had settled in well in the neighbourhood though they didn't see him every day, he would pop round fairly regularly. He had invited them for dinner on Sunday and he would do the cooking, Rose was to sit back and relax for a change.

Rose thought this was so nice of him and she would look forward to it. Angel didn't really feel very comfortable about it at all, there was still something that was stopping her being relaxed around Frank, she wasn't sure what it was.

Rose seemed so excited about it that she would have to keep her thoughts to herself and go and make the most of it. The smell of roast chicken met them in the hallway, the house looked so cosy and welcoming. She could see that he was doing his best to make them welcome and was surprised to feel herself quite relaxed in his company.

Dessert was jelly and ice cream and it was just delicious, reminded her of her childhood and her birthday parties, there was always jelly and ice cream. She thought of Billy, he was so much a part of her childhood that it ached her heart to think of him.

Rose was chatting away with Frank, they got on like a house on fire the pair of them, comparing recipes and ways of cooking potatoes. Frank admitted to being a very plain cook, wasn't rocket science, just ordinary every day cooking, nothing fancy.

Angel excused herself and asked if she could use the bathroom to which Frank answered, there was no need to ask. As she walked along the landing to the bathroom, she passed what she thought must have been his bedroom.

Neat as a pin, there was nothing out of place, in passing, she noticed a picture on his bedside locker, a picture of a baby in the arms of she presumed was the child's mother. It was Moira, her mother and the baby must have been her.

Her feelings of anxiety were never far away, right away she could feel it building up inside of her, she felt like she would choke. Rushing to the bathroom, she breathed slowly and tried to calm herself, after all she knew that Frank and her mother had been together, why she was so shocked that he'd had a photograph of her.

As she returned to the sitting room where Rose and Frank had settled with a glass of wine, Rose had noticed her pale colour and asked if she was alright to which she had answered that she was fine.

She actually felt sick, she knew it was the anxiety, she'd been there before, so she hid it as best she could and didn't spoil the evening for anyone. She so wanted to talk to Frank about her mother and their relationship but it seemed too personal; it would have to be Frank that would be the instigator of that conversation.

As if reading her mind, Frank having gone to the bathroom himself, an hour or so later came into the room holding the framed picture. Trying hard not to look guilty though she could feel her face getting red, she took the photograph from him as he went on to talk about where it came from.

Seems he had taken the photograph at Olivia's christening, as she was called at the time. He had posted it along with a few others to Tom and Moira on his return home. After the tragedy that had left a baby without her mother, Frank had come home to help with the search and came across the photograph that Moira had framed and kept on a table beside her bed.

He stopped for a moment deep in thought then continued, "It's all I have of her now." Both Rose and Angel looked at each other as he went on to say that he hadn't planned on speaking about Moira that evening and that, that wasn't the reason he had asked them over for dinner but as the subject had arisen, maybe it was a good time to talk about her.

He'd also felt that when in their company, as much as he'd avoided the subject, there had always been an elephant in the room! Frank took a deep breath and started to speak, he'd only met Moira a few times before she'd married his brother.

Tom was a high flyer, worked in finance with more qualifications than you could count. The brains of the family, Frank had said with a grin.

His work meant that he travelled a lot, leaving Moira on her own, but that was ok, she'd understood his work was very important to him as she was too obviously. Tom was a gentleman, would do anything for anyone and Moira was mad about him.

They had hoped for a child for many years to the point that it had become an obsession with Moira, it was putting a strain on their marriage and a wedge between them.

Tom had confided in him one night when they had gone for a drink in the local pub, he had been worried that Moira had been drinking too much.

Tom had to go away on business during one of Frank's visits home, it couldn't be cancelled at that late stage and he had apologised to Frank. It was understandable and anyway, it was a very last minute decision to go home, so they hadn't had any warning as such.

He was always made to feel welcome in their home and there was never any question but that he would stay with them when he'd come. It had been a long night of drinking and chatting and Moira had opened her heart to Frank, more than likely helped by the wine!

In trying to console her, things got a bit intimate and one thing had led to another. He'd always admired Moira, she was a beautiful woman, but that was as far as it went. After all, she was his brother's wife, it was a mistake, a big mistake brought on by the influence of drink, or was it.

Did she feel the attraction towards him that he had felt towards her? Turned out they had both felt the same, their meetings became more frequent, he would book into a nearby hotel and she would make an excuse to be with him, or when Tom was away, he would come home for a few days.

It had gone on for a while until the guilt became unbearable for both of them, Moira was never going to leave Tom and Frank was being eaten up inside with guilt. This had to stop, they both agreed, Tom was such a lovely person, he didn't deserve the deceit.

Meeting up with them after that became difficult with Frank, making excuses not to come home to stay with them. When Tom had rang him with the news that Moira was pregnant with their first baby, his heart had sunk.

Moira had told him that it was unlikely that they would ever conceive naturally and Tom wasn't interested in going down any other road but naturally. Hearing how far she was and when the baby was due, he'd put two and two together and had his suspicions alright but that was as far as it could go, he wasn't going to burst their bubble; they were ecstatic with excitement and Moira didn't seem to question it.

That would be that until the day that she wrote the awful letter that she was going to end her life and asked him to look for 'THEIR' baby. Life had taken a turn for the worst that day, what could be so bad that ending one's life became a desirable option, not to mention leaving your child behind!

The rest was history as he had said, he had looked far and wide for the baby he so longed to hold in his arms. The baby called Olivia, whom it seemed no one had seen sight nor light of but he never gave up, she was always at the back of his mind even after all of those years.

Angel, on the other hand, had been pining for her mother, foster parents at a loss as to how to console her until the day that Billy and Rose had taken her home and made a life for her. Rose had got into the conversation at that stage, confirming what Frank had said regarding Angel pining for something.

They could never make out what it was because her background was so vague but she said she remembered how as a toddler, she would sit on the floor playing and when the door would open, she would turn around quickly to see who was coming in as if she was expecting someone.

Looking disappointed when she didn't see whoever it was she was looking for, often a tear rolling down her little face but no outward cry. Rose would go to her and lift her up in her arms to cuddle her but it took a long time before she'd felt that it comforted her.

She remembered watching her sleep at night and asking her as she stroked her beautiful blonde hair, "who are you missing, you poor little girl, who is it you are looking for?" Rose wiped her eyes and apologised, it still upset her.

It was getting late and there had been a lot said and Angel needed to digest it all. Getting up to go, they thanked Frank for the lovely meal and somehow, there was a feeling of calm, the story was out now, there was a weight lifted from all of their shoulders.

This was by no means the end of the conversation, it was just the beginning, Angel was beginning to get to know a bit about her past and about her mother.

It was early to say and she could be very wrong but her mother was beginning to sound a bit selfish, a bit like she didn't care who got hurt, which in this case was Frank, as long as she got what she wanted.

But it was too soon to judge, maybe she'd got it wrong, she hoped she had. They would chat again soon.

Chapter 9
Happy Childhood Memories

On the way home, Rose had left Angel to her thoughts, and as they pulled up outside the house, she apologised to her mother, adding that it was a lot to take in. Rose hoped that hearing Frank's story would maybe fill in a few missing pieces of the jigsaw as it were.

Though she had never discussed her birth mother as such, it had to be at the back of her mind, it was so vague Rose was sure she had to question some things, especially now that Frank was on the scene.

The kettle was put on the boil and they chatted well into the early hours, Angel had no desire to hear about her birth parents, she never had and she was happy to go through life without knowing.

But now, hearing what she had from Frank, it was like opening up a can of worms, thoughts of what they would have been like were crawling like worms out of a can.

Now, she needed to know it all, every single secret that time had held from her, every single moment stolen from her and as she turned the light off to try to get some sleep and maybe stop her mind from racing for a while, she thought of

Billy and the safe easy life she had with both himself and Rose in growing up, she had been so blessed.

Every meeting with Frank from that day on was filled with stories; stories of his brother Tom, a gentleman to the end who passed away not knowing that his wife had been deceiving him and whether she'd known it or not, and Frank felt that she had to have known, she had lied to him that the baby was his, and that by some sort of miracle, they had conceived against the odds.

The more Angel was hearing about Moira, the less she was liking what she had heard, but it was getting more and more obvious that Frank had been in love with her alright.

Cemetery Sunday was a miserable day and Rose hadn't been feeling too good, she had picked up a cold and Angel had suggested she stay at home in the warmth and she herself would go to pay her respects.

There were a few she had to visit there and after hearing the stories about her birth mother, she wasn't really looking forward to visiting that particular grave, but she would out of respect.

Rose had planted some pots for the day, she had cyclamen in pink for Billy's grave because he used to plant them in the garden and she had winter pansies in a few different containers.

She knew that Angel would want to visit Jenny and Brod's grave as she always did and though it was a delicate situation at the moment, she thought she might visit her birth parents Moira and Tom as well, so she planted three pots.

It was hard to get something nice in the shops at that time of year and expensive too, so Rose thought it was a good idea to do the pots herself. She had fully intended going with Angel but really didn't feel up to it, she would go as soon as she felt better.

Angel had gone to Billy's grave first then walked down to Jenny and Brod's, leaving Moira and Tom's until last although having to pass it on the way to Jenny and Brod's. The plants looked lovely in full bloom, brought a brightness to an otherwise dull and dreary day.

She had missed the Cemetery Sunday ceremony intentionally, she just wanted to spend some time alone there, she wasn't into the crowds. A lot of the time looking to see who's grave was left unattended, half of them not praying for the poor souls at all.

Walking back to Moira and Tom's grave, she felt almost sorry for her birth mother; by the sounds of it, she'd had a sad life albeit a short one, as for Tom, she'd had no feelings whatsoever for him.

She'd had no recollection of either of them really, although Rose had said that night in Frank's that as a baby, she'd always looked like she was missing someone, always waiting but she didn't remember.

Her childhood memories were happy ones, happy memories with Rose and Billy. As she turned to leave having left the pot of pansies on the grave, a lady walked over to her.

Looking quite pale and shaken, she spoke with a quiver in her voice, then stopped to take a breath. Angel wasn't sure if she was going to faint or what was wrong. She walked past her and leaned against the headstone, taking a tissue out of her pocket.

"You have to be Moira's daughter, we thought!" Angel listened intently as she went on, "same navy blue eyes, my God, it could be her standing here."

The woman went on to apologise, she had been walking past the grave intending to stop with some flowers when she saw Angel standing there and it was only when she had turned to go that she had gasped.

It had been rumoured that the baby had been saved but no one had ever heard for sure, Moira's friends had assumed that though they hadn't found the baby's body that the worst had happened!

Introducing herself as Tina, she put her hankie in her pocket and walked closer to Angel, looking at her straight in the eyes, there were tears in hers. She put her arms out to hug her, taking Angel by surprise, and she sobbed uncontrollably into her shoulder, her being shorter than Angel in stance.

Apologising for her actions, Angel put her at ease straight away, apart from anything else, she was worried she might get a panic attack, she was so upset. Seems Tina and Angel's birth mother Moira were the best of friends, though not living so close to each other in the later years, they had trained together and were like sisters.

When Moira married Tom, she had moved but they had kept in touch, meeting up with their tales of woe and when there would be any news to share. They would have had so many laughs together, after leaving college, they had shared a flat near the hospital where they had trained as midwives.

Tina had come especially that day to visit Moira's grave for Cemetery Sunday, leave some flowers and reminisce. She hadn't been prepared for what she had seen when she came to the grave though.

"Honest to goodness. I thought I was seeing a ghost," she had said, inviting Angel to join her for a cup of tea and a chat, she was glowing with excitement now that the panic had passed.

Angel agreed to join her and they walked to the nearest coffee shop, leaving the cars at the graveyard, it was easier that way, the coffee shop was only a short distance away and the parking would be easier at the graveyard.

Tina was married with two children, two boys all grown up now, she'd said. One practicing law and the other a bit of a wanderer, liked to travel, thought money grew on trees, however, she'd felt blessed to have them.

Moira, on the other hand, had longed for a child so much, and when she did have a baby, the excitement was something else, Tom was over the moon. Calling her Olivia, as was her birth name, Angel had to tell her that she now went by the name Angel.

Frank had told her a few things about Moira but Tina was now filling in a lot of the blanks, by the time they had finished their conversation, Angel was beginning to feel that she knew Moira all of her life.

She didn't sound like the deceitful woman she had built up in her mind, cheating on her husband and lying to him about her pregnancy. She was beginning to sound like a sad person grieving for the baby she would never have, until Frank came on the scene.

Tina had known about Frank and the affair, Moira had confided in her and sworn to secrecy; she did mention that she had thought that the baby was Frank's. She had cried and cried and said that she didn't want to break Tom's heart, he was so happy.

As far as Frank was concerned, she'd thought he was oblivious to the situation. Frank, on the other hand, had his suspicions but didn't want to upset the applecart. They truly loved each other Moira and Frank, but Tina always thought maybe this relationship all came about through loneliness.

Tom was away a lot with work and that's why Moira had drank so much, she was lonely, Tina said. Frank was always close with both Moira and Tom and she had said she could see it happening and had told Moira as much, a friendly drink, a laugh to kill the time, then a kiss maybe and one thing leads to another!

But she was eager to assure Angel that both her mother and father doted on her, but when Tom died, Moira changed. She sort of went into herself, didn't go back on the drink or anything, just no interest in meeting up or going out.

Tina had said to her even before Tom had died that she seemed a bit down, she remembered the day she said it to her and she'd laughed it off, saying she was just tired that she wasn't getting much sleep with the baby teething.

But Tina was thinking that she might be suffering from postnatal depression, never diagnosed but she could spot the signs. She'd felt that Moira also knew the signs but chose to ignore them and carry on.

Left untreated, PND can go on for a long time and when she'd lost Tom, Tina thought that her whole world fell apart. She struggled to do the smallest thing, when Tina called by unannounced, she would find Moira wearing clothes that looked like she'd slept in them.

She would lose her temper with her baby and cry along with her, it was pathetic, she'd said. The week before the tragedy that had left a baby without a mother and taken a life so young, Tina had asked Moira to move in with her and the boys.

There was plenty of room and the boys were old enough to help out with the baby and give her a break, Tina's husband was agreeable when she told him how she'd found her on the last visit.

Wearing a smile for the neighbours and keeping a front up was wearing her down, she needed a friend though she would never ask for help, she was crying out for it in her face. Agreeing to move in with Tina for a while, Tina had left her that day, content that everything would be ok and arranging to pick her up at the weekend.

Hearing what she had obviously been planning in her head for a while left her devastated. Totally devastated, she would blame herself for not acting sooner. It wasn't that she didn't see that she needed help because she did and she had beaten herself up over it for years after.

Nothing could change that now, Moira had been let down, she had hidden it well and for God knows how long. One never knows what's going on in another person's head. Tina had tears rolling down her face as she sipped her now cold coffee.

She was wound up, hadn't stopped talking since they had sat down. As they parted and went their own separate ways, Tina gave Angel a hug so tight that it left her gasping for breath, she was a big strong woman and had an almighty hug.

Not sure what to say in parting, Angel wasn't sure if it would be appropriate to arrange another meeting, though Tina hadn't mentioned it, only to say she will probably bump into her again at the graveyard.

Though it would break her heart, she'd said to go there, she would go every now and then and every occasion. She would talk to Moira, she'd said, tell her all the gossip as it were just like they used to. As she got into her car, Tina had turned to Angel with a sadness in her eyes.

"Time is the currency of life, spend it well," she'd said and was off down the road. Rose was still in bed when Angel got home, she had been longer than she had planned and hoped Rose wouldn't have been worrying.

She awoke as Angel went into her room as quietly as she could so as not to wake her but she insisted she hadn't been asleep, just resting her eyes. She was no better, in fact Angel thought she looked worse, the sweat was in ripples on her forehead but she wouldn't hear of calling a doctor.

Instead Angel was instructed to go to the corner shop and get some lemons and oranges and a packet of brown sugar. On her return, she was told to boil the fruit with the sugar and leave it on the side of the range from where she would have it warm throughout the day.

She had coughed all night afterwards but whatever was in that concoction, it really worked; she was up and about, still coughing but much better the next day. They talked about Tina and Rose told her it was a pity she didn't bring her back for a cup of tea, she would have loved to have met her.

In hindsight Angel thought that would probably have been a nice thing to do but the thought never entered her head. In talking to Frank about Tina, he had said that her name rang a bell.

Perhaps he'd said that she might have been a bridesmaid at Tom and Moira's wedding, a long time ago now, he'd said but maybe and he wasn't great for remembering names or faces for that matter!

Frank wanted advice on curtains for his kitchen, was hoping Rose might go and pick some out with him whenever it suited; Rose didn't have to be asked twice. The apron was taken off and hung on the back of the kitchen door and she was off into town with Frank.

Angel was so glad that they got along so well, very well in fact, she'd thought. Frank was a lovely man, very ordinary but yet, she still thought of Billy as her dad; she wondered if she would ever feel like that about Frank her biological dad, she didn't think so.

It was so busy at work next day, she longed to get home and put her feet up, maybe she would take a walk in the park at lunchtime, a bit of fresh air might revive her.

She thought of Moira and what Tina had said and how strange that her birth mother had chosen the same career as she herself did, she had always been drawn to that type of work, maybe she'd taken it from her birth mother or maybe not!

All she knew at this time, she thought to herself, was that it was exhausting and the walk wasn't doing much for her either, so she turned back. Tripping over a child's ball, she almost lost her balance and looking up after picking the ball up to hand it to the child who was almost stumbling towards her, holding on to his dad's hand (she presumed) and giggling with excitement.

Could only be a year old, she'd thought, not much older. Clumsily walking his first steps, as she handed him the ball, he smiled a very familiar smile; she'd seen that smile before. Looking up to who was holding his hand, she knew straight away where she had seen that smile, it was on his father's face.

There was no mistaking that they were father and son, none whatsoever. "Lawrence." She smiled at him in disbelief;

surely this wasn't Ralph, who'd lost his mother not long after he was born. Not recognising her for a minute, Lawrence apologised and they chatted for a while, Angel apologising that she would have to get back to work.

She would have loved to chat for another while, see how he was getting on, so she was delighted when he asked her to meet maybe for a coffee in the park sometime, just to catch up.

Lawrence remembered how kind she had been at that awful time of his life, a time that would remain in his memory for the rest of his days. They would meet on her next day off, weather permitting, she had said it was one thing sitting on a bench drinking coffee on a nice sunny day like that day had been but not so inviting if it was raining.

They would make other plans should the weather be unkind. Back at work, she couldn't get Lawrence and his beautiful wife Sybil out of her head and the joy baby Ralph had brought to their lives, short lived, she remembered.

Sybil was so badly lost but who was to know, certainly not the new parents so full of excitement for their new-born that a simple headache could end in disaster for them. She looked forward to meeting them again and hoped the rain would stay away.

Of course it didn't, it had rained all night and it looked like it would more of the same that day. She wondered if Lawrence would have come to the park and didn't want to let him down, so she took her umbrella and walked there in case he would be waiting.

They had said they would make other plans if the weather had let them down but how were they supposed to do that, they had no way of contacting each other and she was sure

Lawrence wasn't going to turn up at the maternity hospital to rearrange things.

She would see the bench from the entrance of the park and it was empty, there was no sign of Lawrence or the baby. There was no need to go further, she hoped they would meet up again by chance maybe, as she turned to go, the wind had taken her umbrella and turned it inside out.

She was soaking wet and struggling when she heard a car horn blow a couple of times from the side of the road. It was Lawrence, he was just parking outside of the park. Agreeing that it wasn't a day for sitting on a bench, he asked her if she wanted to sit in and chat for a while, he had picked up two coffees on the way in the hope that he would meet her.

Getting into the car, she could hear Ralph gurgling in the back of the car, all tucked up in his car seat, he was full of smiles and holding a soft toy, he put it up to his face as if to hide and giggled.

They chatted for the length of her lunch break when she said she would have to get back to work, her jacket dried, by now she hoped she wouldn't get a chill but it was lovely to talk to Lawrence and so nice to see Ralph again.

Such a happy baby, she'd thought, wasn't ignorance pure bliss. Lawrence was doing ok, missed Sybil like hell but was learning to cope and his mother, who he had now moved in with, had been very good to them. He'd thought he had been very lucky to have her.

Angel walked back to work, the rain having stopped by now but she did feel chilly and her clothes felt damp still. While she listened to Lawrence talking, not really getting a word in edgeways herself, she thought to herself maybe he just needed a listening ear.

She hoped it had helped him to talk, he seemed like he was wound up, she reckoned that she could be there still if she didn't have to be back at work. She remembered when poor Jenny and Brod had died many moons ago now, she'd promised herself that she would never get so involved with someone that she couldn't live without them.

Two old people with years of love and memories behind them and the inevitable ahead of them had decided that they couldn't live without each other and obviously had taken it upon themselves that they would never have to face that.

A tragedy, yet an act of true love. Now here was Lawrence, lost without his young wife, going forward only because of their little boy. Not knowing what tomorrow might bring, or if his broken heart might finally fall to pieces, he'd said.

Angel's birth mother again coming into her thoughts, she must have been lost too with no hope at all to do what she done, she'd thought. Life just puzzled her sometimes, why would a mother so young as Sybil with her whole life out ahead of her and her beautiful son and devoted husband, be taken like that, it just didn't make sense.

She was so needed, so very needed. She'd given Lawrence her phone number and told him that she would be there if he ever needed to talk, she didn't want to seem forward but she wanted him to feel that he'd had someone to talk to should he need to.

At going home time, Angel was packing up to go when she was summoned to reception, someone had sent her a bouquet of flowers. Reading the card, she was blinded with tears.

Lawrence had said that it had been their intention to send flowers after they had gone home with baby Ralph, himself and Sybil had intended to do that to thank her for being so attentive and just so nice.

They'd felt that she had gone beyond her duty in being so kind and that they would never forget her. Angel cried all the way home and then some more as she told Rose about her day, she knew that the flowers would have been expensive and that Lawrence wouldn't have had that cash to spare.

After all, she was only doing her job. "It's nice to be appreciated," Rose had said. As she went upstairs to change and shower, the phone rang in the hall.

Lawrence hoped he hadn't embarrassed her by sending the flowers but he'd said it was something that Sybil had wanted to do as well and it felt good to do it, he thanked her for the chat and promised to call her again as long as he wasn't a bother to her.

Angel thanked him for the flowers, though she had said that there was absolutely no need and apart from it being her job to look after Sybil, it was also a pleasure, she was such a kind person that it was easy.

She looked forward to going into work every day, not knowing what the day might bring or who she would meet and have the pleasure to look after. Her's was a very rewarding job though requiring much dedication, she loved it.

Moira came to mind again, she'd thought it strange that she had trained with Tina in midwifery and now here she was doing the exact same thing, very strange!

Rose had arranged to meet Frank for coffee in town and Angel had offered to drop her on the way to work but was delighted to hear that Rose had decided that the walk would do her good.

She had been so into herself since menopause had hit her and hit her hard, that Angel didn't think she would ever see her being confident again. She had lost all of her confidence, fearing the worst if she'd gone anywhere on her own, almost panicking at the thought of it.

Angel had assured her that had she gone to see a doctor that there was plenty of medication out there that would help but her conversation had fallen on deaf ears, she wasn't having any of it.

"What's natural isn't always wonderful," she would say and got on with it. Angel had often seen the panic in her face when they would get into a crowd or maybe if she had suggested a walk, she would always find an excuse not to go.

She was so glad to see her of late returning to the confident person that she always was before menopause. Gradually, she had regained her confidence, walking to the corner shop or going to mass on Sundays, getting into the crowds again.

It was no bother at all to drop her into town on her way to work and normally, she would insist but she wouldn't this time; she would let her make her own way, it was good for her.

Chapter 10
Father's Day

Frank was sitting in the kitchen when Angel got in from work, chatting and laughing with Rose. It was lovely to hear the cheerful banter going on as she hung her coat on the banister of the stairs.

But then Frank was the jolly sort always in good humour, Angel thought, she couldn't ever remember seeing him in a mood. They had spent the morning in town and took the bus as far as the cemetery to visit the graves.

Rose was beaming with joy, she was so pleased to have accomplished a day on her own without feeling panicky, although she had said later that there was a moment in the café that she wanted to run with the rush of adrenaline that she had gotten in her chest but she had learned to breath it out and it had passed as quickly as it came.

She didn't think Frank had even noticed. "Isn't it a man's world too," she had said and they had both laughed. Frank had told her that he had settled well into retirement and the new house, he was so happy to have found Angel and that she had allowed him back into her life.

Angel wondered if maybe she should be making more of an effort in including Frank more in her life. She did see him almost every day and the awkwardness had long passed but yet, she could never look at him as her dad. It was a tough one, Billy would always be her dad as far as she was concerned.

Maybe she would chat with him about her birth mother, there were lots of unanswered questions still and never in a month of Sundays did she think Frank would bring the subject up. Also, she had her birth mother's belongings that Frank had given her that she hadn't even looked at yet.

Well, she had looked briefly a while back but had put it off for another time. It was time, she'd thought, time to bring her birth mother into her life as well.

With no disrespect to Rose or Billy, now such a long time gone, she knew that Rose would support her in anything she wanted to do. Rose, another one that wouldn't bring the subject up in a million years and if anything did come up about Moira, it was like she was walking on eggshells with Angel.

Frank would be invited to dinner; as it happened, it was Father's Day and herself and Rose would go to visit Billy's grave. Rose thought she would do a nice roast and could leave it in the oven while they went, she liked to do it slowly; it would be nice and tender that way.

The house smelled of the cooking on their return and the roast was taken out of the oven and left to rest while the potatoes and vegetables were organised. Angel had also visited Moira and Tom's grave, just out of respect for Tom.

Showing Rose the card she had bought to give to Frank for Father's Day, she had felt a bit apprehensive, she had never really acknowledged the fact that he was her birth father but she was thinking a lot lately about the situation and in a moment of madness maybe, she had strolled into a card shop and picked out a card.

It was very basic just a few words inside, no long verse filled with emotion or anything. But it did say dad on the front! Rose thought it would be fitting to give it to Frank on the day that was, after all, a day to celebrate dads. Angel wasn't sure she would see how the day went.

Dinner was delicious as usual, Rose was such a good cook, it seemed to come naturally to her. The conversation was light and flowing and Angel decided to give Frank the card, she watched as he read it and was happy that she had given it to him, though she had never known him as her father, it didn't change the fact that he actually was.

Frank thanked her and looked emotional but happy. She wasn't even sure if he'd known it was Father's Day. "Sure, there's a day for everything now, isn't there?" Rose had gone to the sink with some dishes and was still talking as she went.

Frank reached out his hand to Angel across the table and squeezed it tightly. "This means a lot," he'd said.

Angel smiled, she'd felt she had moved on a bit and she was glad that she didn't let Father's Day go by, he might not have even noticed but then again, he might!

She hadn't yet addressed him as dad; it was always Frank, maybe someday, she'd thought. For now, it was easier to give him a card to acknowledge it. It was only a cheap card with a few words on it but it had changed everything, Frank was noticeably more attentive though Angel didn't mind a bit and Rose certainly didn't.

It had been ages since Angel had heard from Katie, though inseparable growing up, life had put them on different paths. Katie had called by while Angel had gone to meet Lawrence and Ralph in the park, it was a beautiful day and Lawrence had rang the day before to see if she would like to meet up and have a coffee.

Ralph was now getting stronger in his walking and beginning to run hence the cuts on his knees, Lawrence had said. Angel really enjoyed their company, it was such fun, though she hardly knew them, she always felt relaxed in their company and she'd felt that Lawrence had enjoyed their meetings as well.

There was nothing more than friendship going on as far as she was concerned, though Rose did give her a bit of teasing about them, Lawrence had called by on the odd occasion with Ralph and Rose doted on him.

She was so happy to see Katie on her return though still in a bit of a confused state, Lawrence had asked her if she would accompany him to a gala night being held at his local community hall.

It was a charity do and his mother had been selling the tickets, he thought Angel might like to go. He had caught her on the hop, so she had agreed, not even thinking, not one for going to these things by the time she had got home and had time to think about it, she had got herself in a right old tizzy.

But seeing Katie had put it right out of her head, they chatted for hours, she had given up her job in psychiatry and had taken to travelling. Not yet ready to settle down, she had said and there was nobody special in her life a yet. Asking about Lawrence as Rose had told her where Angel had gone that morning, she too teased her about him.

"A gala night, wow! That sounds serious." Katie was always a devil for teasing. Angel had explained how they had met, thinking about it, she could hardly believe herself that it had been over two years ago now.

"Poor man, how do you cope with something like that?" Katie had sounded sincere and she was, it was a very sad case and only now it seemed that Lawrence was beginning to cope with it.

They had spoken about it over coffee that morning, Angel thought, still tearing up as he spoke about his beloved Sybil and how Ralph had been robbed of knowing his mother. Angel had thought to herself, *me too*.

Though she had been one of the lucky ones in that she had been adopted by the most wonderful couple in Rose and Billy and had never actually missed her birth mother as far as she could remember but she had been robbed of knowing her.

A loss that she had only recently felt in getting to know Frank. Katie would be around for the week and they would get together and go on the town one of the nights, she had said when leaving while winking at Rose at the door.

Knowing full well that a night on the town would never happen with Angel, she just wasn't the sort, never was. But they would certainly have a night out before she went back on her travels and she had invited Rose as well and Frank, if he wanted to come.

Never having met Frank, she had said that she would look forward to meeting him. Angel had told her the whole story, drama and all. She was gobsmacked. "You wouldn't read it in a book," she had said.

Frank was delighted to join them, they had gone to the local pub for a bit to eat and a drink, Katie had chatted to Frank as if she had known him all of her life but then he was such easy company, Angel had thought.

There was no awkwardness about him, he was glad to meet one of Angel's friends as well as someone who'd known her all of her life. He had said that he wished he had known her sooner, his life had changed from being useless to being worthwhile.

He had reached across the table and taken Angel's hand and she had blushed. Katie's eyes had filled with tears and she had excused herself to go to the bathroom.

The week had gone by so fast and Katie would be on her way again, promising to return soon. Rose stood at the front door, waving her off with a tea towel in her flour covered hands, she liked to bake the brown bread early in the day so that it would be nice and cool for teatime.

Frank being the latest fan of her brown bread, she would be baking one for him as well. Angel blew the horn as they took off down the road, she would drop Katie at the bus stop and be on her way to work.

She'd had a few very late nights since Katie's visit and promised that she would get to bed early for the rest of the week. The charity gala night was upon her before she knew it and although she didn't really want to go, Rose had commented on how nice it was of Lawrence to invite her and how it would be good for her to get out for a few hours.

She'd gone through her whole wardrobe, what should one wear to a gala night? She had wondered. Finally deciding on a casual dress not wanting to dress too formal, she ran downstairs to answer the door.

Lawrence stood there, looking very smart in his suit and tie, smiling. He had the most perfect set of teeth and a lovely smile, she was glad she had decided to go although she was tempted to develop a migraine last minute but it was clear that Lawrence had gone to a lot of trouble to look smart.

Now really familiar with each other, he had insisted on her calling him Lal, it was what his friends called him and Rose now too. She could talk till the cows came home, always so friendly and welcoming to anyone who called by.

Frank, now like part of the furniture, would be round in the evening and she would wait up unless it was too late, in which case she would want to hear all about the gala night in the morning.

Angel had looked at Lal and they both went off, laughing. It was a lovely night with music and dancing and finger food being served at every table, they had gone to a lot of trouble. Lal had organised a babysitter for Ralph, a girl down the road that Ralph would know well and should he wake up, he wouldn't feel strange with her.

She had babysat before and Lal was happy to leave her with Ralph. His mother would usually mind him if he was going out or working late but on account of her being on the committee and selling tickets, she had to be there too.

Meeting her for the first time, Angel found her to be very friendly, a lovely lady. Lawrence had introduced her as Maggie and they shook hands and chatted until she was called upon to help with the raffle tickets.

Angel wondered how they would have made much for the charity although there was a big crowd there but the prizes in the raffle and the food would have cost something, she had thought.

In discussing it with Lawrence later in the evening, he had said that the prizes and the food had been donated, so that every penny made on the night went to charity. It had been a lovely night and lying in bed, Angel wondered why she had fretted so much about going in the first place.

Lal was ever the gentleman and treated her kindly as was his nature, she'd thought about Lal and found herself a little excited for the first time in thinking about him, which she'd thought was silly as they were only friends.

Rose was sitting on the bed when she came out of the bathroom next morning, waiting for all of the news about the night before. It was late when they had gotten home and she had gone to bed.

Seeming a little disappointed that there was no news of romance between Lal and Angel, they had both laughed. Whatever would have given her that idea was beyond Angel, neither of them would have shown any feelings of the sort to give her that impression.

She was so glad that it was Sunday though a wet and miserable one outside, all the more reason to stretch on the sofa for the afternoon. She was tired and her feet hurt, she wasn't used to late nights and her shoes didn't help either.

Just beginning to dose off, she jumped as the doorbell startled her. Rose had gone to see Frank, she had invited him to dinner and wondered if he liked sprouts, any excuse, Angel had thought to herself.

They got on like a house on fire, the pair of them did the odd trip to the garden centre and the shops together, it was nice to see Rose heading out and about again. Long enough she had been a prisoner to her thoughts and anxieties that came with menopause.

Before she opened the door, Angel could see that it was Lal at the door through the obscure patterned glass that went three quarters the way down the door.

She'd know his physique anywhere, he was tall of mixed race with his mother being African-American and his father being of French origin. He hadn't spoken about his father much, only that he was French and hadn't been a part of his growing up, so Angel didn't ask.

As he walked past her into the kitchen, she could smell his cologne, probably had only stepped out of the shower. He came round to thank her for accompanying him to the gala night and to say that he had enjoyed her company.

They'd chatted for a while and after a few cups of tea, Lal got up to go, turning back at the door to say that he would like to take her for dinner sometime. Was this more than just friendship? Did he want anything more than friendship?

She wasn't sure but she would take her time and enjoy the moment, she certainly was enjoying Lal's company and even found herself thinking about him when he wasn't there! Rose was coming up the garden path as Lal took off outside the gate, with a devilish look on her face, she walked past Angel and winked.

They talked about him over a cup of tea and Angel told her mother what he had said about going to dinner, not a discussion a girl would normally have with her mother but Rose was different, they had always been very close and it was like talking to a friend, Angel could tell her anything.

Frank came over for dinner and as it turned out, he didn't actually like sprouts, another trait they shared; in fact, as time went on, Angel could see that they shared a lot of mannerisms.

During dinner, Rose had talked about Billy, he certainly was the love of her life, apparent in the way she spoke of him and her eyes that still filled with tears on the mention of his name.

Frank listened with great interest as she went on to talk about how they had fostered Angel and eventually, to their great joy, were allowed to adopt her.

"She brought such happiness to our lives," she'd said.

Frank sat back in his chair and sighed. "Isn't life strange too," he'd said. "Had I known that she had brought such happiness, maybe it would have been easier." it was obvious he too had a story to tell.

Lal was waiting for her outside work with Ralph in his pushchair. Giggling and full of smiles, he was always such a pleasant child. They were going to feed the ducks and wondered if maybe Angel would like to join them, although unannounced, Angel had no plans for the afternoon, so she was happy to tag along.

Ralph wanted to get out of the pushchair as they approached the pond, excited to see the ducks. Lifting him out, Lal took his hand and Ralph reached for Angel's hand, swinging as they walked along.

It seemed so natural, not awkward at all and Lal didn't seem to take any notice either. They fed the ducks and nothing would please Ralph only to name every duck in the pond, it was such a fun afternoon.

Angel thought of Sybil and all that she was missing in his growing up, it didn't seem fair. Neither was it fair that Ralph had never gotten to know his beautiful mother, but then she thought to herself that the same could have been said about herself, Moira looked like a beautiful woman but she had never had the chance to get to know her.

Although different circumstances altogether, the situation was much the same. Moira must have been suffering silently after the loss of her husband to have done such an awful thing, maybe if she had told someone how she was feeling, she might have been there to see her own daughter grow up.

She would definitely have gotten some help to cope, she remembered what Frank had said that day coming out of the graveyard after leaving Moira and Frank's grave. "I hope peace finds her."

It made sense to her now, knowing what had happened back then, her mind must have been a torment to her. Lal was looking at her when she came out of her thoughtful state, smiling, he'd asked her where her thoughts had brought her.

She smiled back and promised him that one day she would tell him but that this day was about Ralph and the naming of the ducks. Just then, Ralph pointed at one of the ducks and said he would call it Angel because it had a smiley face and fuzzy hair.

The wind had blown her hair all over the place and Angel had to laugh at what he had said while at the same time, her heart had fluttered with the joy that was this little boy.

Having arranged to meet for dinner at the weekend, they'd parted company with Ralph reaching out to her to be taken out of his pushchair again.

He was getting to know his freedom now and wanted to be free to run about and not be strapped into a pushchair but as Lal had said, he would take all day to get home, he was a very inquisitive little man, he'd said and there would be lots of stops on the way and questions.

Angel thought about them both over the next few days and discussed her fears and anxieties with Rose about getting too involved. She questioned herself as to whether their friendship would progress to the next level and whether or not she wanted it to.

She didn't want to see anybody getting hurt and especially that little boy, she had told her mother. As usual, Rose had put her mind at ease, assuring her that the future would look after itself, one day at a time, she had said, nobody has tomorrow.

Angel had felt that a weight had lifted from her mind, what was she thinking, it was very early days, she was getting ahead of herself. Perhaps one day, their friendship may progress but for now, she would enjoy their company and not be getting flustered about stuff that might never happen.

Both Lal and Ralph had become regular visitors to the house and Rose was loving it. Ralph too seemed to be enjoying the attention, there would always be something in the sweetie cupboard for him when they called by.

Rose would often take him to the park to enjoy the playground, coming back bursting to tell them about the pirate ship in the playground or Rose had bought him some ice cream on the way home.

It all became very natural for Lal and Ralph to be there so much so that they were now just turning up out of the blue without ringing to say that they would be calling. The bond with Ralph was definitely growing stronger yet it didn't frighten Angel anymore, it seemed right.

Lal would invite her to his house as well and maybe watch a film on the TV or the odd time cook dinner her, he wasn't a bad cook!

As she turned up for dinner on the invitation of Lal's mother, Angel arrived at his house, feeling a bit apprehensive. Though she had met Maggie, Lal's mother, a few times, this would be the first time she had actually sat down to dinner with her.

She needn't have worried, she was so easy to chat to and so very kind. In talking about their backgrounds, both of which were so different, Maggie had gasped at one stage.

"I knew there was something about you, the name, Angel, it took me back and now when you mentioned Rose and Billy, oh! My goodness."

She got up from where she was sitting and gave Angel the tightest hug, explaining that it was such a small world. It was she who took Angel as a social care worker into her office that day.

She who held her when she cried, never knowing what she was crying about, obviously missing her mother. She who dried her tears and combed her beautiful blonde hair. She who took the piece of paper from her pink cardigan with no name on it.

Just 'Look after my angel' hence the name Angel had come about, a name she would never forget. Angel was speechless, she couldn't believe this, she could tell her how when she was placed with Rose and Billy that she would call on her regularly to make sure it was working out, leaving with no doubt that she had been well placed.

Maggie had told her that although she had many dealings with abandoned children, abused children, every kind of family upset, her's was a case that had stayed with her for all of her days working there.

Now retired, she'd often think back and wonder where the children were, if they were happy in life and always hoped that they would have all the luck in the world that any child in that situation deserved.

Angel couldn't wait to tell Rose when she got home, sitting on the end of her bed, she had woken her out of her sleep. In the morning, Rose had asked her if she had dreamed it. But Angel assured her that it was true and that she would invite Maggie over to meet her again after all of those years.

"What a pity Billy isn't here to see her," Rose had said.

Chapter 11
What Was Love Anyway

Maggie was so excited to meet Rose again and Rose likewise, she was so sorry to hear about Billy's passing. They talked for hours while Angel and Lal had taken Ralph to the park, Lal had dropped her off and knowing they'd have a lot to talk about, decided Ralph would enjoy a visit to the park and give them a bit of quiet as well.

Ralph was up to all sorts now and the centre of attraction wherever they went, such a very good looking boy, he could be dressed in rags and still look handsome. Not that he was, he was always dressed in the best of clothes.

It's how his mother would want it, Lal had said one day when Angel remarked on his lovely sailor's suit. Patent black leather shoes and white ankle socks, he'd looked so smart. Lal had said that when they were expecting Ralph, money had been tight, but now with them living with his mother, it was easier, didn't have to stretch it as far so that Ralph could have the best.

As they walked up the path to the front door on their return, they could hear the laughter coming from the kitchen as the window was open. Rose was wiping a tear from her eye with her apron and had put her arms out for Ralph to run to her, which he did without hesitation as Maggie looked on, smiling.

After they had gone, the house seemed so quiet, Angel had never really noticed it before but between Maggie and Ralph, there had been more life in the room than they had for a long time. It was strange, Rose must have noticed it too as she tidied up the table, cups and crumbs and all.

She smiled at Angel and had said how it reminded her of the times before Angel came into her and Billy's life. "Don't children make such a difference!" They both smiled.

Theirs was just a friendly relationship up until now but Lal seemed to be getting more and more involved as in meeting her after work and having her and Rose around to his for tea.

He'd always include Ralph on their days out and Angel could feel herself getting very close to them both. She'd never intended this to happen and she knew that they came as a package. Did she want a readymade family?

That question had come up a few times lately and she didn't have the answer, all she knew now was that Lal and Ralph and even Maggie seemed to have become part of her and Rose's lives and it had just happened that way.

She had questioned the connection with Maggie, how strange that she should be Lal's mother and all those years ago have had a connection with Rose and herself. She was beginning to wonder if what Rose always said was true, that our lives were penned by our God and that we had little control over our destination.

This sure was a strange one and for the first time in her life, she had found herself questioning it. She would never know but one thing she did know was that she was really happy in her life now and felt at last that it had a purpose.

After witnessing the death of Jenny and Brod, she had been left in a state of oblivion, it was like she had been floating from one day to the next, totally lost. Even having met Jenny and Brod and where that had led her, was that not a strange coincidence also?

Her head was reeling from thoughts, she would have to stop thinking and just go with whatever was in store for her in life, she'd felt like she had been carried along with no say in it. Was this possible? Have we no control over it?

As she came into the house after sitting in the car pulled up outside the house for about twenty minutes, Rose had asked her what had her so deep in thought. Laughing it off, she hugged her mother and told her that it was work stuff and that was that. A nice hot bath would put her right, Rose had said and that there was plenty of time before dinner.

She knew he'd had something on his mind as they took off in his car, he wasn't usually so quiet. Not wanting to pry, she would say nothing, he would tell her if there was something to tell.

She hoped it wasn't that there was something wrong, that maybe she'd done something to upset him, surely not. It was quite the opposite in fact, as she discovered when he'd opened the car door as he always did.

Getting down on one knee, he'd produced a beautiful blue stone ring. Angel, totally shocked, gasped for breath and had felt faint. Never in a million years had she suspected or expected this. Lal explained that he'd been thinking about it for a long time, he'd said to have met one beautiful person in

Sybil in a lifetime, he had been so lucky but to have met a second, he had been truly blessed.

He'd hoped that he hadn't overstepped the mark and commented that she was looking very pale. Getting up from his kneeling position, he got back into the car and hugged her. Angel was speechless and wondered if he had taken this as a no to his offer of marriage.

The truth was that he had indeed taken her by surprise, she was shaking but managed a very faint 'yes'. She'd never really thought about Lal in that sense but then maybe she'd thought to herself that this was what love was! Being happy in each other's company, being sad when they're not around!

There was no great romance between them as such, yes, they'd kissed and hugged all of the time but no big show of affection or anything. She had never been in love, so how was she to know what to expect. It felt right and that was all that mattered to her.

Rose was ecstatic on hearing the news, seemingly she knew one day that it would be on the cards, so to speak! Angel had no clue as to how she could have known that, she hadn't seen it coming herself at all.

As the days went on and plans were being made for the wedding, Angel found herself feeling a bit out of her depth. Things were moving way too fast for her, they were to live with Lal's mother as one day that house would be his and it would save them money rather than renting!

There was a wall being built between herself and Lal, mainly made of plans between the mothers. The easy going relationship was all of a sudden a mad rush to get them married. Lal was feeling it too, he was on edge all of the time and they began to argue under the strain.

Angel found herself panicking for no reason, conversations between her mother and herself were all about the wedding. It had got to the stage that she had to put a stop to it all, she was drowning.

Her life was being planned out for her and she wasn't liking it one bit. She had to get off this merry-go-round, her head was reeling. A rollercoaster of emotions, when it should be the happiest time of her life.

She would talk to Rose and explain how she was feeling and she'd felt that Lal was feeling the exact same. Sure, they wanted to spend their lives together but what was the rush, she was only just getting used to being engaged.

Rose was taken aback in hearing how Angel was feeling, she hadn't realised with the excitement of it all. Apologising and assuring her that it was never her or Maggie's intention to take over, she'd said that they'd thought they were just giving them a helping hand.

Lal was so relieved to hear that Angel had the conversation with her mother and he'd intended to do the same. They would move ahead at their own pace and would sort everything out for themselves, if there were problems on the way, they would sort it themselves.

While they had appreciated that the mothers had their best interests at heart, they would now suggest in the nicest of ways that they just sit back and look forward to the future. As for moving in with Maggie, while she was the best in the world, Angel didn't see that happening either.

Rose had confessed that she was sort of relieved to be taking a back seat where the arrangements were concerned, Maggie being an organiser by nature was a bit disappointed but accepted that she too must take a step back. It was a weight lifted off Angel and Lal's shoulders and they had often laughed about it after.

They really didn't want to hurt anybody's feelings but theirs was a life where they relished every moment together, and in time, it would be the right time for them.

Frank had come round for dinner that weekend and Lal had formally asked him for Angel's hand in marriage. He had been so delighted to be asked, saying that he'd thought that asking the father's permission had gone out with the flood.

They'd all laughed and Lal had added that he'd wanted to do things right. Rose and Frank got on like a house on fire, two of the best buddies, had started to help each other in their gardens, go shopping together and as Frank only lived down the street, they would take turns to have coffee in each other's house's throughout the week.

Only just good friends, Rose would laugh and assure Angel that there was no funny business, Billy was her soul mate and no one on earth would ever come close but she was very fond of Frank and appreciated his company.

As he did hers, Frank was a real gentleman, always there to help or advise if it was only which plant went where in the garden. On the odd occasion that they would disagree, it was apparent on Rose's face but they'd never really fall out, Frank would be round with his two chocolate eclairs and all would be well again.

Lal had asked Angel if she would go to visit Sybil's grave with himself and Ralph, he wanted to tell her all about their plans to marry and assure her that he would love her forever. Angel though would never be second best, she would now be his wife and he'd hoped one day, she would be Ralph's mother but that was for time to come.

Angel felt for him as he stood looking at his beautiful young wife's headstone. He'd placed a kiss on his hand and put it on her name and Ralph had done the same. As he wiped a tear from his eye, Ralph looked up at him and held on to his leg, How could a small child understand, Angel thought to herself.

It was evident that he had truly loved Sybil and she had no doubt that he loved her as much, she could never take her place but she would do her best to make them both happy. She had found her path in life and it felt right, Lal had taken time to grieve and had no choice but to move on with a small child to think of.

One day, she'd hoped they could be a family, she knew Sybil would always be a part of their lives and that was ok. Lal had found a place in his heart for her and she would fill it with her love.

Now two years together and Ralph was about to start school, it was a big day for him and he was excited. Lal had said that he had been up since six o clock. Tinged with a little sadness, the day would also bring joy, not having his mother around for the occasion, Maggie had accompanied them to school.

She had been so good to them and often confided in Angel if she had any concerns. Lal wasn't one to open up about his problems and Angel had come to know that in the years that they were together. She would never ask but always knew when something was on his mind.

She knew that Ralph's first day at school would be hard for him, thinking about Sybil but yet, he just got on with it and put on a smile for Ralph, promising to take him for a treat afterwards to celebrate his first day.

He had asked her if she would like to accompany him to school the night before but she had to work and she knew that Maggie would be there and sort of thought it should be so. She was thinking he probably only asked her out of courtesy and not to leave her out, and she wished him luck and wondered if maybe she should mention Sybil.

Deciding not to mention her at that time, she thought that maybe they would take Ralph to her grave after school when she had finished work and show his mother his new school uniform and how smart he looked in it.

Lal had agreed, kissing her on the head and thanking her for being so understanding and caring. Ralph had walked up the pathway and through the school gates without a bother on him, Lal was so proud and Maggie was in tears.

He called Sybil's grave mummy's garden and couldn't wait to leave the flowers there, kissing the red ribbon that tied the beautiful red roses together. Though it had been four years, it was evident that the scars were still tender on Lal's heart, the wound still wept and the pain still gushed.

Not wanting to spoil Ralph's big day, he had just smiled and winked at Angel as she took his hand. Ralph looking so grown up now in his school uniform, so innocent and oblivious to the pain that permeated through every inch of his father's being.

There was much ice cream eaten and treats to take home and have after the dinner. Maggie was cooking his favourite dinner, spaghetti hoops. Angel found herself getting more and more excited at the thought of joining this lovely little family, there was much to look forward to.

Rose and Frank were just arriving from an afternoon's shopping when she got home, offering to help to take the bags in from the car. Frank wouldn't hear of it. Ever the gentleman, he'd already suggested that Rose go in and put the kettle on and he would look after the bags. There were all kinds of goodies bought.

Angel was like a child on shopping day, looking to see what she would eat first. Rose had laughed and commented that she should be watching her figure for her big day. Now feeling a little less rushed about the planning of the wedding, Angel could smile and discuss it with ease.

Lal had suggested maybe a spring wedding the following year and they both agreed that they liked the sound of it. They would start proceedings as soon as Ralph had settled in school, that was the most important thing at that time and seeing as he had settled in right away, there was no reason to hold it off any longer.

Rose and Frank were over the moon, of course there was the issue of where they would live afterwards. Frank had a suggestion but it would have to be something they'd wanted themselves.

Money was of no issue. Frank had seen to it that Angel was comfortable in that area, so investing in a property of their own wasn't out of the question, only there were no properties available within miles of where they were and there was Ralph's school to think.

So, Frank had said if they wanted to, they could build on his land, his property had come with planning to build a similar sized property in the garden, a huge garden way too much for his creaking bones to look after. It was perfect!

It was near to Ralph's school, near to Rose who she didn't want to be too far away from and a stone's throw from Lal's mother as well. Too excited, she had to ring Lal to discuss it with him there and then, he had no hesitation in saying yes and would get the ball rolling straight away.

Angel had come back into the kitchen, glowing with enthusiasm, she'd hugged her father and thanked him, promising not to invade his privacy and not to be a bother. Frank replying that his house would be hers someday anyway, had said that it was his pleasure to help them out.

The smile on her face was enough thanks for him, at last he could do something for his daughter whose life he had mostly missed out on, whose mother was the love of his life. He felt good and Rose was so happy as well.

Angel hoped that Maggie would understand that they wanted their own place and be happy for them too. Ralph couldn't contain his excitement and Lal's only regret was that he had mentioned it to his mother within earshot of Ralph and just before his bedtime.

He had been washing the dishes while Ralph played on the floor for a few minutes before his bedtime with Maggie clearing the table after the dinner. After hanging up the phone to Angel, she'd known by his face that he'd had news.

She was delighted, it would suit everybody and everybody would be close by. It was a great idea, she had said while Ralph had jumped up and down, asking when he could move into his new house and if he could have dinosaurs on his bedroom wall and sparkly lights on his ceiling.

Like stars, he had said, "mummy can watch me while I am sleeping then, from the stars." Lal had no doubt but that Sybil was already watching him and always would.

It had been a sort of comfort to him always, though he wouldn't say that he had great belief or anything but from what he had witnessed in watching Ralph growing, he was convinced that there was definitely something, they weren't alone!

They would wed in the old abbey down the road and have a small reception afterwards in the hotel in town. There wasn't much choice as to where to hold the reception that being the only hotel nearby and they didn't want to have to travel miles for it.

It would suit them perfectly, there wouldn't be a big crowd anyway, they both preferred it small and personal. Katie, her best friend, would be her maid of honour and Frank would give her away.

Maggie and Rose would walk Ralph up the aisle, holding his hands one each side of him, more to keep him from being giddy than anything else but it would be nice. He was so excited to get dressed up like his dad in a suit and dickie bow that he could hardly wait for the day.

It was coming round fast too, Angel was beginning to get the nerves. She was sure of what she was doing and she now could firmly say that she did love Lal and wanted to spend the rest of her life with him, so why was she so nervous and anxious as the day approached.

Rose assured her that every bride is nervous as the big day gets nearer, she'd said that she remembered when she'd married Billy, she was so nervous that she couldn't stop shaking and nearly didn't get there.

But was she glad she did, although a life together cut short, it was a life that had brought so much happiness, enough to bring her through the rest of her life without him, though she would have loved for him to have seen Angel on her wedding day.

Her dress was pure white, almost crisp to touch and rustled as she walked. She had decided against wearing a veil, just a simple band of flowers in her hair, Rose had given her a blue handkerchief that had belonged to Billy.

"Something old and something blue," she had said with a tear in her eye; happy tears, she had said.

A simple thing but Angel would hold it to her heart forever. It had rained all night but the sky appeared to clear, though it was cold, Angel didn't notice. Her heart was racing as she got out of the car at the chapel.

Ralph had broken loose from Maggie's grasp and ran to her, hugging her with great difficulty, trying to get his arms around her dress, as Maggie shouted at him to come back. Angel took him in her arms and smiled at him.

He wasn't worried about soiling her beautiful dress with his wet shoes or almost knocking her over with his rush to greet her. He was a little boy, living in the moment as children do, never thinking of the outcome of their actions.

Angel was just so touched by his show of affection that soiling her dress was the last thing on her mind and all of a sudden, her nerves disappeared. She walked up the aisle, smiling, with Katie dressed in a burnt orange dress ahead of her, and Maggie and Rose holding on to Ralph with all of their might, walking ahead of Katie.

Lal stood at the altar, dressed in his suit and dickie bow, looking very handsome and smiling as Ralph came towards him. Katie took Angel's bouquet and Frank, looking smart in his suit, proudly handed her over to Lal and shook his hand.

This was the sort that day dreams were made of, Angel thought to herself, looking around her, the only thing missing was Billy. There was a seat left vacant on both sides of the chapel, one for Billy and the other for Sybil with flowers left on both.

Lal took her hand and kissed it, he looked so happy. Angel hoped that he could see the joy in her eyes too, a joy coming straight from her heart. She had been so excited that she'd nearly forgotten to breathe and felt a bit faint but nobody had noticed and it passed.

The ceremony over and the celebrations on the way, Lal had told Angel that she had made him very happy, and that he'd felt so lucky to have found happiness again.

Chapter 12
The Landlady and the Lodger

He'd appreciated how Angel had always included Sybil in their lives and had said that she had such a big heart. Angel had always thought that this was the right thing to do; after all, she was Ralph's mother and she had felt honoured to be a part of his growing up.

She could never take his mother's place but she would do her best to fill the void. A mother can never be replaced, she'd thought. Just then, she'd thought of Moira and Tom, she wondered if Frank was thinking of them too, he was looking a bit sad.

There was a strange feeling in her heart and she wanted to share it with Frank, so she asked if he would like to dance with his daughter on her wedding day. She'd cried on his shoulder, unnoticed by anyone around on the dance floor with the lights sort of dimmed.

She wasn't sure why she was crying, it just happened, she couldn't explain her feelings but she was feeling lonely. As if understanding in that moment, Frank held her tighter and she was sure that she had heard a sniffle from him too.

The day had gone off without a hitch, they would go away together for a couple of days alone, not long enough for Ralph to miss them, though Maggie had assured them that he would be fine and she'd loved spoiling him.

It was a lovely couple of days. Angel had never felt so happy and content, whatever doubts she'd had on the morning of her wedding must have been nerves like Rose had said. She really had felt a bit apprehensive that morning but as the day went on and she'd stood outside the chapel, she knew it was the right thing to do, there were no doubts.

Theirs wasn't a mad love affair nor was it a marriage of convenience and she had questioned herself many times after Lal had proposed, was it convenient for him in his circumstances with a small child to bring up on his own?

But throughout their time together, his kindness and caring ways, it was very plain to see that Lal did truly love her and her him. Be it a familiar kind of love where friendship was their foundation or a love that had indeed come about through tragedy, which really and truly it was.

It was something they'd both wanted and she couldn't be happier, she'd thought. She'd often questioned her journey in life, how different things had happened down through the years to have her change direction.

She thought of Billy and what he would have said of her taking on a readymade family and she knew exactly what he might have said. He would have told her to be happy and that was all that was important in life.

Love starting out in a relationship isn't the same as the love one feels when together for a long time. Love grows with every moment you spend together. Billy was never one to believe in love at first sight, he just couldn't understand how two people who knew nothing about each other could fall in love at first sight.

Of course, there was the attraction at first but he believed that attraction alone was a very shaky foundation to build a relationship on, let alone a marriage. As Ralph ran excitedly to Rose's front door, he'd almost tripped over the step and fell into her arms as she stood there.

She had been waiting for them to call, though it had only been a couple of days, she had missed them. Apparently, Ralph had missed her too, he'd hugged her and held onto her hand as they headed to the kitchen.

After a glass of lemonade and far too many chocolate biscuits, Ralph had curled up on the sofa and fallen asleep. "Too much excitement for one day," Lal had said and carried him out to the car, he would take him back to his mother's house for a nap and Angel would stay behind with Rose and have a catch up.

Still awaiting an engineer, they would stay with Maggie for a while as it would be less unsettling on Ralph. Frank arrived just as Lal pulled away from the pavement with a big hug for Angel, he seemed excited to see her.

Looking at Rose and winking, Angel just knew the pair of them were up to something. Sitting her down, he began to tell her that Rose was thinking of taking in a lodger but that she wanted to see what Angel thought of it first.

She had been thinking about it since she knew that Angel would be married and she didn't relish the thought of living on her own. She'd always had someone to make a bit of noise about the place and she couldn't bear the quiet.

Angel had thought a lot about her mother living on her own and dreaded the thought, so she was delighted to hear of her thinking about taking in a lodger as long as it was someone nice and she was happy about it.

Sniggering between themselves, they'd told Angel that the lodger would be someone they both knew and looking at the way the two of them were going on, it didn't take much to guess who she was talking about.

Frank had said that they didn't see the point in both of them rattling about in two empty houses and it had made more sense for them to share. There would be no funny business, Rose had assured her, Frank insisted that he would pay his way and it was mostly for the company.

Angel thought it was a great idea and yet, there was another surprise in store for her, Frank was signing his house over to her and Lal, so that there would be no need to build after all.

It would only be a matter of time before it was hers anyway. "Why wait," he'd said. Angel was flabbergasted when Lal came back to collect her with Ralph sleeping soundly in his bed.

He couldn't believe it, the generosity of her father to even think of doing such a thing. They would do a few bits to make it their own and it meant that they would have their own home in no time at all.

He couldn't thank Frank enough and they hoped that things would work out for himself and Rose as landlady and lodger. Sure, they got on like a house on fire.

Rose seemed so happy, they were actually very compatible, not in a romantic sort of a way by any means but they looked out for each other and had great respect for each other's privacy, so it had worked out beautifully.

Lal had been busy decorating Ralph's new bedroom and Ralph had made his own mark on it too, without being told to do so, Ralph had put his hands into the tin of paint and pressed them onto the wall where his dad was painting.

At first, Lal had told him that he shouldn't have put his hands into the paint but in looking at it later, Angel thought it looked cool. He'd put his own mark on the place and in years to come, when they'd look back and see the imprint of his tiny hands, it would bring such good memories.

Moving in day had come at last and though Maggie had been so good to them, they had longed to have their own place, there hadn't been much to do with Frank's house as he had kept it very clean and tidy himself, just a few bits and pieces.

They would have Rose and Frank and Maggie of course, round for dinner to celebrate the move. Angel was beside herself with excitement so much so that she'd actually felt ill. Rose had brought flowers and Frank came with a bottle of wine and Maggie had baked an apple tart for dessert.

There was plenty of chat throughout the dinner and everybody seemed to enjoy themselves, Maggie had wished them the best of luck as she got up to go. "You know what they say," she had said as she walked towards the door, "new house, new baby."

They all laughed but Angel had noticed that Lal was looking a bit concerned. Of course, they hadn't thought of how Lal was feeling on that subject, he was bound to have bad memories of when his beautiful Sybil had gotten so sick after the joy of having their baby.

Angel wasn't sure that he would ever want to go through a pregnancy again, he had never mentioned children. It just never came up and Angel hadn't given it much thought up to then either.

Lal would walk Maggie home only a stone's throw in one direction and Rose and Frank only a stone's throw in the other. It was the ideal situation, they would never be short of a babysitter with so much family around, or a cup of sugar even. Angel was very happy with the way things had turned out.

With all the fuss of late and the moving in and all of that, Angel hadn't taken any notice but when she was feeling ill again the following morning, the penny had dropped. Could she be pregnant?

Alarms had started to go off and she couldn't wait to get out of work and do a test. Would she be happy or sad, she wasn't sure, it wasn't something she had planned and Lal, would he be happy or would it bring the sadness of the past to the fore again?

Struggling to get the key into the door, she'd raced to the bathroom, her hands shaking, she'd actually felt afraid. Her daily job saw new babies brought into the world with no bother, just plain joy but what if she was pregnant and something were to happen to her. What if?

Before she had a chance to take the test out of her bag, there was a knock on the door, it was Maggie with Ralph, he'd picked up some bug or other in school and all he wanted was to be at home with his teddy bear and a cuddle from Angel.

Maggie had commented that Angel didn't look so good herself and that maybe she had picked something up as well. Offering to stay and look after Ralph, who was happy now once he was at home, Angel was concerned that Maggie might pick up the bug as well and she didn't want that.

Thanking her, she'd walked her to the gate and came in to find Ralph almost asleep on the sofa, which wasn't a bit like him. She'd covered him with a blanket and let him sleep for a while, going back into the bathroom to do her test.

It was clear as day she was going to have a baby, with gasping breath, she threw cold water over her face; she was in shock. How could she tell Lal this, what would his reaction be. They were so happy with their little family. Would this upset the applecart?

Ralph had called out and she would have to tend to him, she would have to keep this to herself until she'd had a good think about it.

Not that she would ever think of not having her baby but she wanted to suss out what Lal might think, but then she'd thought to herself, she hadn't given him a chance, maybe he would be delighted and then she could be delighted as well. She would tell him when Ralph was in bed and settled.

Lal was over the moon. Angel had never seen him so excited, why did she think he wouldn't be? They had talked half the night, mentioning Sybil as well and Angel was glad that he had mentioned her.

This was very close to the bone and he had to have been brought back to that awful tragic time. Angel was so terribly sick the following morning that Lal had taken the day off to look after Ralph, he was still a bit poorly with the bug, it was a struggle to get fluids into him and he was starting to burn up.

Lal was panicking and Angel wasn't much help to him hanging over the sink, she had managed to leave the sink long enough to put a cold face cloth on Ralph's forehead and had given him some ice in a glass.

With the heat of his hand, it wasn't long melting into lovely cold water and the novelty of watching the ice melt and sipping the cold water through a straw meant that he was getting hydrated.

Panic over, Lal had read him a story and pampered him all afternoon while Angel, having made an excuse not to go into work, had relaxed as well. Rose and Frank and Maggie were all so delighted to hear the news.

Rose had hugged Angel so tight and Angel just knew that they were both thinking along the same lines. "If only Billy was here," time had gone by so quickly and the pregnancy so smoothly that before she knew it, Angel was on the verge of giving birth.

Having worked as a midwife and experienced all sorts of deliveries, she'd thought that she more than anyone would be well prepared. Wow! Was she in for a shock, the labour went on into the early hours having started early that morning.

Awoken early in the morning with the discomfort, she'd just put it down to eating too much the night before, she just couldn't get comfortable, so she'd got out of bed and walked across the landing to check on Ralph, who was sleeping like a baby. Lal too had been sound asleep and hadn't heard her get out of the bed.

She'd gone down to the kitchen to get a drink and decided to put the kettle on and make a cup of tea when she'd felt the gush of water that she couldn't control.

Having plenty of knowledge of childbirth, she knew that she would have time yet, so she decided to run a warm bath. The contractions had started just as she got out of the bath, so she awoke Lal who had jumped out of the bed and was struggling to get his leg into his trousers.

It had made her laugh, assuring him that there was no major panic and that she would have hours yet, she asked that he would take Ralph to his mother's. Watching him with Ralph going down the pathway, she wondered what the poor child was thinking, he'd looked back and blown her a kiss as Lal took his hand.

It was a normal school day as far as he was concerned, they would fill him in later. Rose was on the doorstep five minutes after Angel called her with Frank trailing behind, she herself was about the only one not panicking.

The labour was tough and long, Lal had stayed by her side not that he was of any real help but at least he was there. A beautiful little girl was born and for a moment, Angel thought of Moira, wondering if her labour had been as hard for her when she was born.

What would she think of her granddaughter and Tom, her husband, what would he think? She thought of Frank and how he must have felt when she had been born, knowing in his heart that she was his daughter, yet not there at the birth and watching his brother's joy on her arrival.

She would have to have a really good chat with Frank once things settled down, there was a lot she didn't know about Moira and Tom and he was the only link to her past. Lal had left it up to her to name their daughter, although they had many discussions over the pregnancy but hadn't settled on a name.

"We'll know when we see her," they had agreed but while Lal had gone to collect Ralph from school to bring him to meet his little sister, Angel had a thought. In fact, she had been thinking it for a while now.

Lal's eyes had lit up when she told him on his return, they would call her Sybil, after Ralph's mother and Rose, after her own mother, the only mother she had known. Rose was so delighted that she'd cried all the way home, Frank had said.

Angel hadn't bounced back as quickly as she thought she might and had spent a lot of time sleeping while the baby slept. It was exhausting, she had never felt so tired. Rose would call round every day to help out and Maggie would collect Ralph from school and keep him at her house until Lal came from work.

Fed and watered and ready for bed, Angel knew she was so lucky to have such lovely family around her and she sure appreciated it. She wondered if maybe her birth mother had such support would things have worked out differently.

Her hormones were all over the place, bringing questions into her head that had frightened her at times and she'd begun to understand why Moira might have taken her own life.

Having a young baby was tough enough but losing her husband on top of it would have been devastating, she must have hidden it well, Angel thought, until she could take no more.

Frank had said a few words on his first visit to Moira's grave that would stick in her head forever. "I hope peace finds her." She wasn't sure if it was her hormones or the fact that she now knew the lows as well as the highs of giving birth.

One thing she did know was that she wanted to visit Moira's grave, she wanted to introduce her daughter to her birth grandmother and it was a feeling filled with urgency at that moment.

Frank had offered to take her while Rose would wait at the house for Ralph to come home. It was a moment of deep emotion, somehow she was feeling a real connection to her birth mother.

Like she wanted to hug her and apologise for not being there when she'd needed support. Frank too had spoken about Moira, a devoted mother, who was crazy about her daughter but smothering in the tidal wave that was grief.

Her mind had been a torment to her, he had said, guilt, lies, deceit and he had been partly to blame. Their attraction to one another was way too strong for both of them and the drink didn't help either, he'd said and then gasped, "If I had known about the demons that haunted her—" He'd cried openly like a child.

Moira would have been a wonderful mother, he had said and walked ahead of Angel, leaving behind the love of his life, and the brother all those years ago that he had deceived.

Pulling up outside the house, Ralph came running down the pathway, bursting with excitement. "Sybil got a present. Sybil got a present," gently rubbing her face as Angel began to take her from her car seat, he'd smiled and said, "I'm going to call you Billy, not Sybil."

Angel was taken aback. "Billy?" Where did that come from, she'd thought to herself and smiled, maybe he was with her today! Katie had posted a gift, for 'Mother and Baby' the card had read.

Ralph couldn't contain himself with excitement to open it. It was a beautiful baby photo album that read 'Welcome Baby' written in gold writing with a cream lacy cover.

Angel had smiled, she missed Katie so much, she would treasure it and fill it with beautiful memories as Sybil grew up and when Katie would visit, she could catch up on all the different stages of her growing that she had missed.

It was a very thoughtful present from a very dear friend. As Sybil got older and grew into her own personality, the name Billy had stuck. Angel thought it actually suited her, she was full of the devil and herself and Ralph got on like a house on fire.

Though nearly five years her elder, Ralph would play with her and was very protective of her, it was funny to watch them sometimes and having two grandmothers living nearby, they were spoilt for choice.

Whether it be ice cream at Nanny Maggie's house or Nanny Rose's biscuit jar with the latter being the most popular. Life was good, Angel had given up her job after Sybil was born and was enjoying every minute of being a stay at home mum.

Lal would call her a home maker, he was so appreciative of everything she'd do and she was so happy to do it. It had given her time to stroll to her mother's house and sit and have a cup of tea and a chat, she'd felt so lucky to be able to afford to stay at home and raise her family with ease and to be able to give of her time generously.

This too was down to her birth mother, she had provided for her, though tragically giving her choices in life where others didn't have them. She thought about Moira every day and often wondered what it would be like, had she been around.

Rose too had often spoken about Moira, seemed she and Frank would often chat and Moira's name had come up a few times. In listening to Frank, she had come to pity Moira, it sounded like she had been so alone and at her wits end after losing her husband.

"The poor woman. I hope she's at peace now," she'd said. Rose had been the best mother Angel could have asked for and now looked like being as good a grandmother. She doted on the children and couldn't get enough of them, insisting that Angel and Lal have a night out at the weekend for a break and she and Frank were only too happy to watch the children and put them to bed.

Maggie, on the other hand, would have the children all day long but was nervous of having them at night, in case anything would happen to them. Lal had told her that his mother had trained as a nurse in her young days and went on to do social care later on.

She'd never explained why until Sybil died and it had brought it all back to her, seems while she was on night duty one night, there was a child admitted with a fever and he was placed in her care through the night.

Suspected to have meningitis and waiting on test results, he was a very ill little boy and she didn't take her eyes off him once until a junior nurse came along to let her have her break. When she'd come back on the ward, there was an awful commotion, the child had had a seizure and was now put on life support.

A desperate decision had to be made by the poor boy's parents to let him go when they were told that everything had been done for him and there was no hope. Though not her fault or in any way her negligence, she would carry that guilt with her and eventually decide to change her career to a less responsible role as a result. It had left her fearful of the night and still did, she'd hated the darkness.

Angel had listened with her mouth open, thinking does one ever know what's going on in another's mind, their fears and demons. Maggie was lucky to have Lal, though having to rear him single handily when the dad had decided that there was more to life than changing nappies and was off for himself, never to return or make contact.

Chapter 13
The Diary

In moving her stuff, Angel had come across a suitcase of Moira's belongings that Frank had given to her all those years ago, she'd had a quick look through them and put them back into the suitcase again and hadn't looked at them since.

Ralph had gone to school and baby Sybil or 'Billy' as she was called now, was having a nap, so Angel decided she would go through her mother's belongings and sort them for once and for all, it was time.

There were bits of jewellery, a couple of ornamental bits, which she had wondered why Frank would store them for her. Nothing that would really give her a sense of her birth mother. Nevertheless, she wasn't going to part with them, not now anyway.

As she put the stuff back into the suitcase, promising that next time she would sort them properly, something had fallen on the floor. It was the diary, Angel had forgotten about the diary and she gasped and picked it up, it was the closest she had gotten to her birth mother, would it hold any information that would make her feel real?

Up to now, she was just a name in Angel's mind, yet something was gnawing at her mind, something telling her that there was more that she should know. Checking in on baby Billy who was sound asleep, Angel decided to open up the diary; if nothing else, she would see her mother's handwriting.

She could have written it herself, it was the exact same handwriting, all the little squiggles and everything. Angel found this amazing, maybe she did have some of her mother's traits after all.

There were different entries of different occasions of her life, at first Angel had felt that she was intruding, it read very emotional at times.

Frank had been spoken about as in Moira's feelings for him and how she was in love with two men. She'd spoken about her longing for a child and had entered every date of her negative tests in it and there were many.

She had written about her anger and frustration, it was like she was self-analysing herself and seemed to Angel that Moira had been struggling long before Tom had died or even before she was born!

Being almost three quarters full, Angel would go to it with every spare moment she had, it had given her a true insight into her birth mother's life, or rather, her life's story thus far. Her mind seemed in turmoil, she'd suffered panic attacks and told nobody about them, only to enter it into her diary dated with the wording, "It's happened again."

Angel knew that Frank had to know more about Moira, he'd told her many stories but mostly happy ones, he'd never gone into the true story, which was evident in her writing, that she was depressed.

She'd needed help and obviously had hidden it well, perhaps had hidden it from Frank too and even Tom. Maybe

Frank hadn't realised the extent of her problems and then again, maybe he wanted Angel to remember her mother as happy. She would never know, she wouldn't be showing the diary to anyone, it was bad enough herself intruding on Moira's privacy, she wouldn't bring it any further.

As she came to the end of the entries with only half a dozen blank pages left to write, she'd almost felt sad, it was like she was there with her mother, hearing all of her stories first hand like she had been discussing her fears with her, which unfortunately wasn't true.

As she put the diary into her bedside locker, a note fell from the back of it, she hadn't noticed it as she read it but there was a little pocket on the inside of the leather cover and she reckoned it must have fallen out of there when she moved. It was a letter written by her birth mother to her. 'Darling Olivia'.

"Oh my goodness!" Angel started to shake, it was a letter for her from her mother. As she began to read it, she'd cried out loud, it was too hard, she would go over to Rose when Lal came home and read it with her.

Of course, she would tell Lal about it too but just not yet, he would understand and support her in any way that he could.

Rose was amazed to hear that first of all, Angel had plucked up the courage to read the diary and though a very private matter, she had confided in her to read it with her. The paper was frail but the ink was as good as the day it had been written, Angel thought. Taking a deep breath and having Rose by her side, she began.

"To my darling Olivia." Her hands already shaking, she'd gone on with a quiver in her voice.

"If you are reading this letter, then I take it that you are all grown up and beautiful. I am so glad that it got to you as it was a long shot that it might. I am such a mess, my darling and I wanted you to have a better life than what I could offer you.

"My days are filled with fear and anxiety. I have no one to turn to and when you cry, it frightens me so much." Angel had to stop for a moment to breath. "I know what you must be thinking by now that I was a selfish person leaving you in the hands of strangers but I didn't know what else I could do.

"In fact my darling, it was probably the most unselfish thing that I ever did—believe me, I did you a favour—what life would you have had with a mother like me. I tried so hard and cried every day, knowing what was looming.

"I couldn't see any other way. I promise you, this is so hard but I am a prisoner in my own body. I fear going outside in case I get weak or sick or die. I am constantly thinking about dying. I just can't take anymore.

"Please forgive me Olivia, my beautiful Olivia; my demons have taken over and now there is nothing left for me to do, only to muster up enough courage to take you somewhere safe.

"I feel like the walls are closing in on me and I am out in a sweat but I will make it to the car and do this very last thing for you; know that I love you with all of my heart, my darling and be happy.

"I will take my demons with me, so that they cannot ruin anybody else's life." The letter was signed, 'Mama'.

Rose watched her daughter's heart break right in front of her eyes and there wasn't a thing that she could do to prevent it, this day was always going to come, she knew that and she was glad to be the one to hold her tight until the moment had passed.

Lal was so sympathetic towards her as well she'd already told him her story and always hoped that she would find closure, now at last he'd thought she had. Her birth mother sounded very troubled, he'd said and that she was to be pitied and that it was just such a shame that she didn't get the help she'd needed at the time but time had moved on now and she had been badly lost.

With empathy in his voice, he had said, "Times winged chariot was drawing near when she wrote that letter." Somehow having read her diary, Angel had begun to understand why her mother had left her and taken her own life, it hadn't made it any easier but she'd felt she sort of understood it better.

Lal suggested maybe taking some flowers to the grave at the weekend and taking the children to visit their grandmother. It was a beautiful day and really warm, Angel didn't know if it was the heat or the fact that she hadn't eaten that morning but she'd felt really watery as they came closer to Moira and Tom's grave.

She could have thrown up as she leaned forward to put the flowers on the grave. She'd been so emotional since she'd read her mother's letter, or suicide note rather. That's what it was really, she'd thought, what an awful state of mind to be in with nothing but doom and gloom on your mind and walking around in fear and pure darkness.

The more she'd thought about it, the more scared she was getting, what if she had inherited her mother's depression; what if one day she would have feelings like that, it scared the hell out of her.

Lal, noticing that she was looking very pale, had taken her hand to help her up and that was enough to assure her that even if she did inherit her mother's depression, she would have the support that her mother never had by the sounds of it.

Over the years, she had come to depend on this man and knew without a doubt that he would always be there to support her. God help her, Moira had fallen down into a dark hole and couldn't see any way out, she wasn't responsible for her actions nor in any way to blame.

Angel felt at peace with her at last and actually pitied her mother. Tom, without a doubt, would have been a loving father though not her birth father.

Looking at Frank she knew this, brothers would be alike in their ways and Frank was ever the gentleman, warm and caring, he'd take the coat off his back and give it to you. Angel just knew Tom would have been the same.

She wondered if maybe baby Billy had taken her mischievous character from Moira or Tom, she certainly was full of the devil, would run rings around Ralph. Still not feeling the best, Angel had asked Rose if she would mind having Billy for an hour or two and looking at her face, she was only too delighted, herself and Frank would take her to feed the ducks.

Billy was all excited and couldn't wait for Angel to go, so that they could go to feed the ducks. It was a massive surprise to find out that she was expecting another baby, though Billy was now toddling around and no bother at all.

Angel had been contemplating returning to work once she was in school. That would be out of the question now, Lal was over the moon, it was the best news he'd heard all day, he'd said.

She hadn't discussed going back to work with Lal at that stage as it would be a while off yet anyway but in a way, she felt a bit disappointed but such is life, she'd thought. She too was ecstatic about having another baby though not planned, it would be wonderful.

The thought was going around in her head for weeks before she was due to give birth, if it was a girl, she would like to call her Moira after her birth mother. She would discuss it with Lal and see what he thought, it would be a way of including her in their everyday life.

If it was a boy, maybe they could call him Tom. It was an easy labour compared to her first and it was a girl, a beautiful girl who could have been a spit out of her mouth, she looked so like herself.

The nurses were coming in and out to see her as it was the talk of the maternity ward, no one had ever seen a baby to look so like its mother. Angel had been told that she also looked very like her own mother, it was like she was reborn and now, a part of her life again.

Moira Olivia she was christened, bringing to mind a part of her past that was once lost forever.

Rose wanted to go to Billy's grave and bring some flowers from her garden, it was the first thing she'd do when her garden came into bloom every spring. Frank offered to take her in his car and maybe Angel would like to come too with the kiddies.

He'd always called her children 'the kiddies' and had often said that he was so grateful to be a part of their lives.

Angel took the children across the graveyard to visit Jenny and Brod's grave, a lifetime ago now, she'd thought.

Thinking back on her rounds and all the lovely people she'd met and got to know, she wondered if any of them were still around. Ralph chased a rabbit that had come out of a bush and Billy went tearing after him and Angel just sighed, she had been so blessed.

With baby Moira gurgling and looking up at her from her pram, she had so much to tell her when she was old enough. Time and tide waits for no man that was so true, we must live every day and appreciate, nobody has tomorrow and it's a very thin line.

Her birth mother Moira, one woman so overthrown with grief and depression, had affected and still affected so many lives.

She would remain in her memory forever, her photo given to Angel by Frank would stand in her kitchen for all to see and her children would be told that their nana was with the angels and Tom.

Rose and Frank, like an old married couple, would go on to be best friends and housemates and Maggie would always be there for support. Lal and Angel would appreciate all of the support that they had around them and never take it for granted.

Ralph's mother Sybil would be remembered in their daily lives, so that Ralph would grow up knowing that he was much loved. Some days, Angel found it hard not having her work to go to, she did enjoy it and loved meeting people.

It wasn't the money or independence of it all, her mother had seen to it that she could choose to do whatever she wanted, she just missed her colleagues and the busy days with no one day the same as another.

Perhaps, in the future, she would pick up where she'd left off and then again, she'd thought having time was nice too; it was only some days that it bothered her.